WHISPERING
WOODS

WHISPERING WOODS

L.C. Markland

Whispering Woods

Copyright © 2021 by L.C. Markland. All rights reserved.

No part of this publication may be reproduced, stored in a retrieval system or transmitted in any way by any means, electronic, mechanical, photocopy, recording or otherwise without the prior permission of the author except as provided by USA copyright law.

The opinions expressed by the author are not necessarily those of URLink Print and Media.

1603 Capitol Ave., Suite 310 Cheyenne, Wyoming USA 82001
1-888-980-6523 | admin@urlinkpublishing.com

URLink Print and Media is committed to excellence in the publishing industry.

Book design copyright © 2021 by URLink Print and Media. All rights reserved.

Published in the United States of America

Library of Congress Control Number: 2021903039
ISBN 978-1-64753-684-8 (Paperback)
ISBN 978-1-64753-685-5 (Digital)

01.02.21

CONTENTS

Acknowledgments vii
Author's Note ix
The Whispering Woods xi
Introduction xiii
Chapter 1 1
Chapter 2 6
Chapter 3 10
Chapter 4 14
Chapter 5 17
Chapter 6 21
Chapter 7 24
Chapter 8 30
Chapter 9 32
Chapter 10 34
Chapter 11 37
Chapter 12 40
Chapter 13 45
Chapter 14 49
Chapter 15 53
Chapter 16 60
Chapter 17 64
Chapter 18 67
Chapter 19 71
Chapter 20 75
Chapter 21 80
Chapter 22 84
Chapter 23 87
About the Author 95

ACKNOWLEDGMENTS

The Whispering Woods is my seventh novel. My other works include: *All Things Work Together for Good (Romans 8:28), Winds of Change, Hard to Say I'm Sorry, Whispers in the Willows, Killing Me Softly,* and *No Holds Barred: No Holding Back.* Though two of the novels, *All Things Work Together for Good (Romans 8:28)* and *No Holds Barred: No Holding Back,* lend themselves to sequels, this one has definitely been written for future series.

It would be wrong for me to underestimate the power of encouragement. In 2014, I stepped down from my position as a pastor. At that time, I was plagued with pain as four back surgeries ultimately took their toll. My physical and emotional well-being were taxed beyond their limits. During such time, some friends encouraged me to start writing. Sure, I threatened and even entertained the thought, but I never anticipated or even expected to write one, let alone seven.

Though my inspiration came from some great friends, it was my mother, Lucy Markland, who planted the seeds. She loved to read. In fact, she read every genre imaginable. My enthusiasm for literature stems from her. She always wanted to write a novel, but she didn't. She believed she lacked the education and experience to do so.

When she passed away, I promised to pen a story on paper. What I didn't know was how that vow would come to true fruition. For twenty plus years, I grew accustomed to sharing stories with others. It's what I did. But the stories I told had already been told. It was for me to study them and then verbally share them to others. To begin a book from the beginning and see it through to the very end seemed virtually impossible.

That's where some friends stepped in. They encouraged and even enticed me to pursue the dreams of my mother. They went so far as to support me along the way, whether it was proofing my work for content and errors or financially supporting this endeavor. Diligently, they gave of their time and resources. Faithfully, they have walked with me. Their motivation for me to push forward, motivated me. They are: Judy Markland (my wife), Janice Erb (mother-in-law), Peter Markland (twin brother), Shirley Rice Verhey (a true friend), Jim Neidert and Raymond Shook (fellow high school graduates), and Tara Boice. I would be remiss not to acknowledge Leslie A. Matheny for co-authoring three of the novels written. They are *Killing Me Softly*, *Whispers in the Willows*, and *Hard to Say I'm Sorry*. She, in her own right, deserves special thanks.

I dedicate this work to Lyndon J. Markland. Before I started working on this piece, he unexpectedly passed away. Shortly before his death, he proved himself to be a valuable friend and brother. Never did I know the impact my works had on him or his life, nor did I know that it was his passing that would prompt me to return to the position I stepped down from.

AUTHOR'S NOTE

The Whispering Woods is a culmination of my education in criminology, victimology, and my experiences in counseling. Of all novels, this one in particular is different from my previous books.

It is a murder mystery. Though the majority of the book is fictional, the details regarding serial killers are facts. Certain characteristics are defined and described based on interviews with those who had an appetite to kill and the means and measures they used to conceal their crimes.

While writing this work, I was reminded of several verses found in Scriptures. Two of the most prominent thoughts are found in the book of Numbers 32:23 which declares, "But if you do not do so, then take note, you have sinned against the LORD; and be sure your sin will find you out (NKJV)," and the second is discovered by the prophet Jeremiah. In chapter 17 and verse 9, this Old Testament prophet dictates that, "The heart is deceitful above all things, and desperately wicked. Who can know it (NKJV?)?"

As you read, The Whispering Woods, let me encourage you, the reader, to be mindful of the quotes cited above. Realize that we, as fallen creatures, are capable of doing the unthinkable and the incomprehensible. Whether we want to accept that our crimes carry less weight than others, in the eyes of God, all sin is punishable by death.

Yet, regardless of the weight any sin carries, God is a gracious God. He has provided and paved a way for us to be forgiven and pardoned. He has done so through his son, Christ Jesus. In the book of Romans, Paul reminds his readers that *the wages of sin is death, but the gift of God is eternal life in Christ Jesus our Lord (6:23, NKJV).*

In advance, I thank you for taking time out to read the work provided below. I pray you enjoy the story as it has been written. I also pray that you are blessed to read it as I was to write it.

Sincerely,
    L. C. Markland

THE WHISPERING WOODS

by L. C. Markland
Review by Raymond Shook, April 2017

The *Whispering Woods* is the seventh novel by L. C. Markland. This novella is a mystery, and the first one of its genre by the author. Through L. C. Markland's previous works, biblical scripture and references are incorporated into the stories, and the author continues this practice with *The Whispering Woods*.

The introduction focuses on the murder case of Becky, a young woman found in the basement of her family home. Becky's father was convicted of the crime and received a death sentence. This case is personal and professional for most of the protagonists and antagonists in this story. Meghan Mitchell was Becky's best friend and is a police detective who works with her father, known only as the chief of police, a.k.a. the Chief. They cooperate and compete with the antagonists: the media in the collective sense and Scott Oliver who is a very successful and a celebrated detective. He was brought in by the Chief to help solve high-profile murder cases. Becky's murder, investigation, and her father's conviction and sentencing influenced the Mitchell family to relocate to a much smaller community. By the end of the introduction and within months after settling into their new town and police department, both the Chief and Meghan are confronted with the recent discovery of a graveyard of twenty murder victims.

Detective Oliver is once again brought in to help the Mitchells find the murderers.

As the story continues, time works against the detectives to find the murderer. Outside and inside pressures bring suspicion to several characters. There are a few twists and turns, but this story focuses on character interactions. In between the interactions are memories of Becky, her family, her murder case, and its results. L. C. Markland really pushes a "past is prologue" agenda in this work.

In general, *The Whispering Woods* is a quick read but has a way that jars the reader. There is a feeling that something is not quite right, that missing pieces are yet to be discovered, and that encourages the reader to carefully push on. Matters are not completely resolved in this story, leading for the reader to want more stories in the near future. But given the nature of feelings elicited by this novel, one must ask if they want that emotional cavalcade. If the reader is brave or the type that enjoys being thrilled, then there is a desire for L. C. Markland to shock us again as soon as possible.

INTRODUCTION

Meghan Mitchell is a young detective. She was born and bred to enforce the law. Her father was a devoted chief, and her mother was a high-profile attorney. Whereas it was her father's duty to uphold the law, it was her mother's to defend it.

Tragedy hits home when Meghan's best friend, Becky, was found dead. Becky's body was discovered in, of all places, her basement. Her final resting place was a 50-gallon drum. Meghan's father recruited the services of a renowned detective by the name of Scott Oliver. Detective Oliver was the best of the best. His interest in pursuing criminals peaked when the national spotlight shined on two serial killers: The Son of Sam and Ted Bundy.

Oliver wasted no time in sniffing out the perpetrator. Sadly, it was Becky's father, a good friend and fellow officer to the chief. Meghan's mother did her best to represent him, though she had reservations about the father's guilt. In the end, he was convicted and condemned to die.

The trauma was too much for Meghan's family. The chief could not grasp that Becky died on his watch and that her father was the killer. The mother struggled with the verdict and poor Meghan blamed herself. She was, after all, the last person to see her friend alive. To prevent the family from enduring another scandal, the family left the city and moved to the suburbs. The chief accepted a position in a small town where murder was unheard of, the mother continued to practice and protect the law, and Meghan was driven to follow in her father's footsteps.

Unfortunately, the community was plagued when Little Johnny, a young boy in the neighborhood, disappeared. His body was found months later in a nearby ravine. To complicate matters, his fragile frame was not the only body discovered. In total, nineteen other bodies were found in the base of this ravine. The killer sent a letter to the police and press on the precise day when Becky's father was to be executed.

The chief recruited Detective Oliver to assist Detective Mitchell. The decision to combine the two detectives was comparable to mixing water with oil. They are incompatible. Both detectives have their own agendas and their own suspicions. Trust becomes an issue when the evidence points to everyone involved.

In the end, everything is up for grabs. Nothing is definitively resolved.

While there are hints that identify the killer, it is for the reader to decide.

CHAPTER

1

The wind gently whistled through the woods. Clouds slowly made their way across the sky, blanketing the sun from casting its warm rays to the land below. Occasionally, the sun proved its power as it found a broken seam within the cloud's lining. The golden glow it showered upon the earth was nothing more than breathtaking. The leaves, also, were in full fashion as their differing colors skirted the skyline and littered the ground. The animals were busy preparing for the season soon to come. Birds were either busy packing their bags to travel south or were bunking down in their nests. Squirrels scurried across the foliage collecting the nuts needed to survive the season ahead. Deer silently pranced through the thickened woods in search for a soulmate.

Everything worked in perfect harmony. This picturesque scene was given to man as a reminder of God's creative handiwork. The clouds added to this majestic portrait as they unleashed a fury of flurries. The flakes that once gently fell from the heavens gained in strength and size. The leaves that once blanketed the barren soil were now buried. Treetops that once lined the skyline with their colors were now laced in white. They beheld the beauty of nature.

It was in this winter wonderland that these woods would cry out its deepest and darkest secrets. It was in the peace of this paradise where the birds built their nests, the squirrels scurried, and the deers danced that the sins of the past would be unearthed. For it was on this day that two young teenagers, Paul and Carl, would stumble upon a shallow grave that lay at the base of a steep ravine that separated the remotest part of the woods from the rest of civilization. At its bottom was a steady flowing stream that flourished during the spring and, at times, froze during the winter. It was this stream that supplied the animals with the water to survive. And it was this stream where Little Johnny's lifeless and partially nude body remained hidden for months.

Johnny disappeared during the first week of June. It was the end of another school year, and Little Johnny had high hopes of spending much of the summer with his sidekick, Danny. He was last seen riding his bike through the neighborhood that resided outside of the park. Neighbors reported seeing him. He was heading toward Danny's house when an unmarked vehicle was seen roaming the streets. Believing it was a police car, they thought nothing of it. By their standards, their community was a great place to raise a family.

It was located in the suburbs. It had everything to offer: parks, ballfields, a local pool, an excellent educational system coupled with a strong local government. But most importantly, it had people who honestly cared for one another. Crime was literally unheard of. When Johnny vanished into thin air, most people were not really concerned. In as far as they knew, Little Johnny's imagination got the best of him. They reasoned that he decided to either go on some great adventure the wilderness offered, or he went on a solo mission seeking to capture the "bad guys" as he always exclaimed.

Never in a million years did anyone think that some harm may come to him. It was something that did not happen in this neck of woods. But it would be something that would come to haunt the residents of this small rural town. When the sun started to bid its final farewells to the day, Johnny was nowhere to be found. His parents, though optimistic, walked the streets looking for their only child. Door to door they went asking the residents if they had any knowledge as to where their Little Johnny may be found only to be turned away.

Frantic soon turned into fear. When news started to spread throughout the community, teams were formed to find this little guy. People broke up into teams scouring the terrain. Some searched the streets while others scoured the woods. No one, unfortunately, dared to scale the steep slope of the ravine. And who could blame them? Little Johnny was last seen riding his bike. He knew very well the dangers that loomed if he rode his bike near the edge.

Darkness soon enveloped the stillness this June evening offered and the hearts of everyone. Johnny was missing. Was he lost? No one knew. Was he hurt? No one knew that either. His parents walked home in despair. Such despair was added when it dawned upon them that their Little Johnny was not there. His father, Henry, picked up the phone to do the unthinkable and unbelievable. He phoned local law enforcement to report that his Little Johnny was missing. His mother, Cindy, walked to Johnny's room, laid on his bed, and prayed.

Her prayers for peace and protection over her little boy were quickly drowned by the steady flow of tears that effortlessly streamed down to her lips.

Henry quietly walked to Johnny's room. Like Cindy, he, too, was numb. He opened the door to Little Johnny's room and laid next to Cindy. He was beyond words. Unlike Cindy, he could not find the words to speak or even utter. Prayer, though important to him, was beyond his grasp. He wrapped his right arm around her and joined her in the orchestra of tears.

The last time he sobbed so hard was during Johnny's birth. For years, he and Cindy tried to have a child. Sadly, they were met with misfortune as each pregnancy miscarried. Little Johnny was their last hope of having the family they so desperately desired. When Cindy's pregnancy with Johnny reached its second trimester, they celebrated the life that was now within their reach.

In a moment of weakness, Henry blurted out the question they both wanted and needed to know. "Why?" The answers to this question were too difficult for them to digest. To know that their little boy was out there alone tormented them. All they could do was wonder if their Little Johnny needed their help, if he was crying out to them, and where he was. All they could do was wonder.

The doorbell broke the silence. It was the officer called to investigate Little Johnny's disappearance.

Henry quickly wiped the tears from his eyes. He tried to regain whatever composure he lost. In a moment of haste, he ran to the door only to find an officer standing before him. It was a young female officer. All she could do was question everything about Henry's little boy. But when push came to shove, there was nothing she could do until morning. It was dark and practically impossible to find a young boy who, at times, sought adventure in the wilderness that laid behind the peripheries or who sought to catch some criminal terrorizing the neighborhood.

CHAPTER

2

That evening could not move any slower than what the hands of time could permit. Seconds turned into minutes, minutes turned into hours, and hours...well, there was no stopping time.

The local news team caught wind of Little Johnny's disappearance. People from the surrounding counties joined the search. They spent days looking under every nook and cranny. In the end, their efforts proved futile. Unbelievably, no one bothered to look down the deep ravine where Little Johnny's body was finally put to rest. Like his parents, most people believed he would never dare go near the edge of such a steep bank. If only had they known. But time has a way of rectifying the wrongs of yesteryear.

The officer in charge of the case was Meghan Mitchell. Officer Mitchell was a hometown girl. Her father was the police chief of this local suburbia not known to most folks. Her mother was a high-profile attorney in the city situated beyond the horizon.

As a little girl, Meghan always inspired to be a police officer. Her interests in police work heightened before her family migrated to this remote place barely noticeable on the map. Her father was the chief of police when her best friend, Becky, was abducted. Her fragile frame was not discovered for some time. Her remains were stashed and somewhat sealed in a 50-gallon container. As fate would have it, a gas leak prompted the authorities to investigate the dwellings when neighbors complained about a "foul odor" permeating through the cracks of this basement.

When the gas company investigated the complaint, the representative immediately realized the smell was not a breach in the line but rather escaped through contents of this partially sealed drum. He quickly notified his superiors and then the local police. It was then that Becky's end came to full fruition. After her body was officially identified, the coroner reported that her precious life came to a tragic end. She was raped and beaten with a foreign object. The cause of death was asphyxiation by strangulation.

Meghan's father felt like a failure. It was his job to "serve and protect," yet a young girl disappeared and died by the hands of some monster on his watch. To make matters worse, that monster was Becky's father, who happened to be a personal friend of the chief and a fellow officer. It was then that Meghan's father opted to patrol a community where life was more simplistic. Never could he see himself enduring another endeavor of this magnitude.

To complicate matters, Meghan's mother was summoned to represent the defendant. She had her suspicions: those suspicions were founded on the lack of substantial evidence. In the course of the investigations, the crime scene unit failed to produce the gold necklace her parents gave her for her tenth birthday. Though many investigators, particularly Oliver, believed Becky's father stashed it as some trophy,

Meghan's mother thought differently. As such, she requested for another attorney to preside over the hearing. Her pleas were ignored. The community demanded that justice be done, and the court was determined to mete out that justice. She had no choice but to defend this one-time friend and fellow officer. The circumstantial evidence was overwhelming. Everything pointed to Becky's father. As such, the guilty verdict was rendered before the trial commenced. The father was sentenced to death. It was a sentence he readily accepted. He remained silent throughout his trial. Most people equated his silence to a "matter of guilt." But in his eyes, life without his little girl was not worth living.

As such, Meghan's parents always aspired that their little girl pursue another field outside of law enforcement. But then again, aspirations are exactly what they proclaim to be- aspirations. Traumatized by the events that led up to Becky's disappearance and death, Meghan vowed never to allow another child to disappear and die. Her dream was to fight crime and prevent another tragedy.

And who could blame her. Meghan had everything required to be a "crime fighter." She had the intelligence. Since both parents were intertwined with law enforcement, she had an innate instinct to be an excellent detective. For as long as she could remember, Meghan attentively listened to her parents discuss cases. Life in the big city was demanding and, ofttimes, dangerous. There was always some commotion: a murder, a robbery, drug trafficking, gang violence, and the list goes on. You name it, Meghan heard about it. From the very beginning of a high-profile case to its end, Meghan listened and learned.

Her athleticism equaled her academics. Because of Becky's death, Meghan committed her life to regimens of exercise and healthy living. She blamed herself for Becky's demise. Had Meghan not left Becky on that fateful day, Becky may have very well been spared the horrors from her father's hands.

For years, Meghan held herself to a higher standard. She needed to prove herself. She needed to exceed and succeed. Her parents achieved a high profile within the surrounding community and city abroad. To further complicate matters, Meghan's mental and physical wherewithal would be put to the test. She was, of course, the only woman in a police department dominated by men. From the police academy to becoming a detective, some of her colleagues didn't feel she could handle the day-to-day duties, stress, physical attributes, and the toils of what an officer goes through on a daily basis. In fact, many officers believed she moved up the ranks more so because of her father rather than her own personal gifts. Over time, she proved to be just as capable as any male counterpart within the force.

Little Johnny's disappearance would put her skills to the test. When his remains were discovered, her father called in some reinforcement. He called an old-timer to help oversee Meghan. A detective who had both the experience and education to solve this crime. He summoned Scott Oliver to the case.

CHAPTER

3

Scott Oliver was a seasoned detective. Twenty of his thirty years of service was spent in investigating homicide. His resume and reputation were beyond reproach. He was a man of action. His instincts were feline in fashion. Like a leopard that sneaks on its unsuspecting prey, Detective Oliver silently sought and stalked criminals. He had a knack for hunting anyone down. If any detective could smell a rat, it was Scott Oliver.

His repertoire included several high-profile cases. The media eventually dubbed him, The Stealth.

His fascination for becoming a homicide detective started when he was a boy. He grew up in Brooklyn, New York during the seventies. At that time, a serial killer by the pen name Son of Sam was running the streets. He shocked the city, as well as the country. His modus operandi was shooting his .44 caliber pistol at young couples while they sat in their cars. In the end, six people perished while seven victims had to endure the psychological and physical pain wrought by his shooting spree. For months, the Son of Sam teased the police department. He mailed letters to the local papers and police taunting them to catch him.

Finally, a much-needed tip led law officials to his apartment building. It was there that he was apprehended and then arrested. Surprisingly, he was more than amicable to admit that, yes, he was the Son of Sam. He smirked as he went into graphic detail as to how he was able to paralyze the people of New York and stump the police department for so long. His reasons for his onslaught was farfetched and frightening. During an interview, the Son of Sam claimed to be following commands from a demon that rested in a neighbor's dog named Sam.

According to the Son of Sam, the dog would bark out commands for him to kill. He argued that he did everything to stop the voices. He even went so far as to shoot the dog but was unsuccessful. The dog survived the malicious attack thereby clinching its power over the Son of Sam. There was nothing he could do but to succumb and surrender to the strong grip this so-called demon of a dog had over him.

Scott Oliver's interest in law enforcement reached its peak when another serial killer soon made the news. Unlike the Son of Sam, this predator was charming, intelligent, and extremely handsome. Born to a single mother, Theodore Cowell was considered a "bastard" by his classmates. Socially, he was awkward at best. He spent most of his time to himself. Scholastically, he was smart. He attended college and even earned his spot with a prestigious law school.

Though his stepfather legally adopted him, where he took on the name *Ted Bundy*, he could never shake off the hurt brought on by the stigma others assigned to him. Eventually, he targeted women who reminded him of his mother. They were young and attractive. They had long dark hair, and they all had firm builds. Later, many criminologists would argue that his choice for this particular breed was the result of being raised as a "bastard" compounded by a broken heart he endured in college.

At the time, he stayed under the radar. His crimes were sporadic and were separated by state lines. To further confuse authorities, this madman used different tactics and techniques to terminate life. He would either strangle his victims, stab them, or beat them until they drew their last breath.

Despite his best efforts, he could not conceal his impulses. There were some commonalities to the thirty-six murders he confessed to. In each case, he would prey on the conscience of his victims. He often masked his true motives by pretending to be impaired. Once he set his sights on his next casualty, he would cry out for assistance. His charisma and good looks earned him their trust. Before his victims knew it, they were in danger. It was too late. Like a rag doll, he would clutch each woman, throw her in his vehicle, and take them to some remote place. He proceeded to violate each girl in indescribable ways. When finished, he would either mutilate or decapitate his trophies. Some believe he often frequented his conquest where he would relive each episode.

It was not until he finally failed to finish an assault that authorities started to connect the dots. Detectives from around the country conglomerated and found striking similarities between this mass murderer and other unsolved murders within their jurisdictions. During his trial, Ted Bundy cast his final assault and attack on society. In a last-ditch effort to spare his own life, he denied any legal counsel only to serve as his own attorney.

In many ways, he gained the national attention he so craved. News crews from around the country gathered outside the courthouse to report on his trial. Regardless of his crimes, people were mesmerized by what they saw and heard. Young Scott Oliver was one such person. He followed the case from its beginning to its end.

The sensations of both cases caught Oliver's interest. He knew that his future would someday be fighting crime. Whether he desired the national attention gained through such cases or the adrenaline associated with the hunt, he did not know. All he knew is that one day he would be famous.

CHAPTER

4

Meghan was at the crime scene when she first met Scott Oliver. Though she heard her father speak highly of him, she didn't recall ever meeting him. Her first encounter with this man of fame and acclaim was not received very well. Initially, Meghan felt threatened and intimidated by his presence.

But then again, Detective Oliver did not help matters much. He started to bark out orders to the officers on the scene.

"Tape off the perimeter!" he commanded. He then countered with, "Make sure you label every piece of trace evidence!" Finally, he asked, "Who is the officer in charge? I need to speak to him."

Meghan was appalled. She was taken aback by such a derogatory comment. "I am!" she spouted. "And who in the hell do you think you are?"

"I am Detective Oliver! I was requested by your chief to oversee this scene."

How could he? she thought. Her mind then drifted to the past. She remembered how helpless she felt when Becky's body was discovered. She also recounted how it was Detective Oliver who ultimately broke the case wide open.

She had mixed feelings. On one hand, Meghan believed her father undermined her ability to solve this particular crime. On the other hand, she knew of Detective Oliver's reputation. He was, after all, a legend. Detective work was his legacy.

Detective Oliver was quick to draw her mind back to the case at hand. "My apologies, Detective," he said somewhat sympathetically. "I did not know that a woman was called to lead this investigation. And who might you be?"

"I am Detective Meghan Mitchell."

"Meghan Mitchell?" Detective Oliver said with a half-hearted smile. "You mean Chief Mitchell's little girl?"

In an attempt to regain some control over her authority, Meghan shot back, "Yes, I am his daughter, but a little girl I am not."

"My, my, my!" Detective Oliver blurted out. "You have definitely grown into a woman." Putting his right hand above his right knee, he continued, "You were this tall the last time I saw you."

Well, if Meghan was to earn his respect, her next statement worked. "Look!" she exclaimed. "Are you here to help solve this case or catch up on the past? If it's the latter, then you need to move on your merry way and let us do our job!"

Oliver burst in laughter. "Well, I can tell that the apple did not fall too far from the tree. You are definitely a Mitchell."

His laughter and comment came to an abrupt stop when an officer surveying the crime scene ran to the detectives. "We have a real problem here," he said while trying to come up with the words to say.

Detective Mitchell and Oliver shouted in unison, "Well, officer? What is it?!" Their voices reverberated throughout the ravine. Everyone paused to hear what this officer had to say.

"Well..." he stuttered. "You see..." Words escaped him. He was speechless.

Again, both detectives tried to find the cause for such an alarm. Another officer finished what the first officer could not, "I believe you both need to take a look at this."

"At what?" they asked.

"I think it's best you come to see for yourselves. Follow me," he whispered and whimpered. What the officers had stumbled on, but could not say, was beyond words. The ravine that remained off-limits had become a landfill of decomposing bodies. At present, five other bodies were found.

Meghan could not grasp the full extent of what she saw. Again, her mind rushed back to Becky. She recalled overhearing every detail of Becky's final moments. To think, no, to know that others had suffered the same fate was too much for her. She broke. She buried her head in the chest of the detective she initially dismissed.

Oliver remained composed. This was not the first time he stumbled on such a sight. As a senior officer, he did everything to continue the investigation. His instincts dictated that there were more bodies, and yes, more victims. He did what was expected of him. He instructed his officers to continue their search of the ravine, all the while offering comfort to his new partner, Meghan Mitchell.

"Come on," he whispered in Meghan's ear. "Let's get out of here and go to the station."

CHAPTER

5

The drive to the station was silent. It was somber. Meghan's mind spiraled out of control. To know that six bodies had been retrieved and possibly more was too much for her to stomach. Sure, she had seen photos of various crime scenes and read about each one. But this was a far cry difference. This was more personal. It was before her. There was no backing out. Her true ambition in life was to serve and protect. That is: to prevent crimes before they occurred, not to solve them.

Detective Oliver, knowing the gravity of the situation, took the fifth amendment. He remained silent. He wanted and waited to see what other details were known about the case. He had a hunch that this serial killer would ultimately notify the public of his misconduct and misdeeds.

His hunch was correct. By the time both detectives made it to the police station, word of the day's event spread through this small town community. They did not have a chance to regain their thoughts or composure when Chief Mitchell blurted out, "We have a serious problem!"

"We know, Chief," Detective Oliver replied. "Tell us something new."

"It's worse than you think," the chief responded with his head hanging down.

"How in God's great creation can it be any worse?" Detective Meghan snapped back.

"I need you both in my office, pronto!" the Chief snorted.

The two detectives followed the chief to his office. Chief Mitchell could not help but slam the door. He walked behind his desk only to throw out what the local newspapers had printed as well as a personal note from the serial killer. The front page of that morning's paper read: "Catch Me If You Can!"

Apparently, the perpetrator notified the news agencies across the country and the police department. He gave explicit details as to what they should find and where to find it. According to the letter, officials should find nineteen victims at the base of the ravine. This serial killer also gave a description of every victim, as well as every means and method implored to end each life. The crime for each murder occurred in different jurisdictions, thereby making it almost impossible for officials to note any similarities between them.

To further confuse officials, the letter was identical. The "perp" used different fonts and styles from various magazines and articles to write the letters. This "perp" also made sure there were no identifiable markers, such as fingerprints and DNA.

Before the police department could respond, the newspapers had already printed the letter. The townspeople flooded the phone lines inquiring about the frontpage news. They wanted to know: How was it that journalists knew about the crimes before local law enforcement? Their concerns were legitimate. What they did not know was how these murders occurred over a great period of time and how each victim came from different localities, different races, different ages, and different professions.

The hunt was now on. Detective Oliver's adrenaline kicked in, while the chief and Detective Mitchell remained still. Meghan was stupefied. She had no clue as to what she got herself involved in and with. She wanted to be strong, yet the sorrow over Becky's death still haunted her. She planted her head in the chief's shoulder and sobbed.

"If it's a hunt he wants, then it's a hunt we will give him," Oliver shouted.

"Chief, I want the reports from the coroner's office as soon as possible. Detective Mitchell, now is not the time to cry on your daddy's shoulder. We have work to do!"

"Where do we go from here?" she quietly asked.

The chief broke the stronghold he had on his daughter. He broke his silence as well. "I left the big city to get away from crap like this..." He stopped for a moment and sullenly stared into the eyes of his now lead detective. Oliver knew exactly what the chief was thinking. The emotional and psychological wounds from the past were as fresh as the day Becky's body was found. Her death remained in the hearts of the chief and Meghan.

And who could blame them? Of all days to find Little Johnny along with a host of other lifeless companions, it was this day. It was the twentieth anniversary of Becky's father's verdict.

"Is this some kind of sick joke?" the chief shouted. "Twenty bodies in twenty years...how can that be?" He paused for a moment. Something about this scene struck him as odd. "This cannot be a coincidence," he murmured.

Detective Oliver reminded his new recruit that there was much to be done prior to the autopsy reports. The first and foremost was to find out where these letters originated. The second thing was to find out the names of the missing persons.

"If we could find out who the victims were and where they came from," he said, "then we have a place to start our investigation."

"Go!" the chief said to his detectives. "Detective Oliver is to be trusted. He knows what he is doing. Go and find this madman." He pulled the chair out from behind his desk, sat down, and asked they shut the door. Overwhelmed would be an understatement. The chief was baffled beyond description. He was lost. He crossed his arms, buried his head, and sobbed.

Eventually, his time alone was like his spirit. It was broken. His secretary burst through the door only to inform the chief of his press conference in fifteen minutes.

With his head still resting in his arms, he nodded and softly thanked her. "Twenty bodies in twenty years, all on my watch. How am I going to explain this to the victims' families?"

CHAPTER

6

The detectives left the station and proceeded back to the crime scene. The woods that once cried out to God's creation now cried out for justice. It beckoned to return to the days of old. It, the woods, had been stripped of its innocence. People would no longer remember it for the joy it represented, but for the remorse it was soon to impart. What was, at one time, the glory of God became nothing more than a graveyard. Lives were lost. Blood was shed. Blood was spilled. There was no turning back.

The woods would never be the same. The birds remained perched high in their nests. Squirrels sought refuge in another part of the woods, and the deer no longer danced through the thickets. The snow could not hide the secrets that laid buried beneath its cover. Nature had been disrupted.

Like the woods, people were also raped of the peace and solitude their community once offered. The street was literally littered with news crews, investigators from the FBI, the sheriff's department, state troopers, and the local police department. This small town was no longer secluded, but was a national spectacle.

Despite the negative attention, people, like a magnet, were drawn to the sensation. They tried to get a glimpse of the bodies escorted up the steep ravine. It was not until a small body bag made its way up the hill that they realized the severity of the situation. It was Little Johnny's remains. There was a hush in the air. People drew deep breaths when a strong wind kicked up from nowhere.

Detectives Oliver and Mitchell fought their way through the crowds. They scaled down the deep bank that robbed the woods of its richness and the community of its reputation. At the bottom of the hill, they saw Johnny's parents speaking with an FBI agent.

They were struggling to keep their composure. Who could blame them? Their little boy was bludgeoned. He was brutalized. Detective Oliver interjected between federal agents and Johnny's parents. Most detectives would be shunned if they even thought of such an attempt, but then again, this was Detective Oliver. He did, of course, have a reputation for breaking some of America's greatest cases.

Clearing his throat, he sympathetically asked, "Is there anything we can do for you?"

Johnny's father, maintaining what composure he could, said, "No, no, thank you."

"Sir, I have to ask you this question," Oliver continued. "Are you sure the body recovered was your little boy's?"

Cindy, clutching to her husband, answered, "Yes." Pausing for a moment, she attempted to continue her statement. "Yes, yes it was, but he is…" With that, she broke down in tears.

Detective Mitchell joined the conversation. "Cindy, Johnny was?"

She mustered what strength she had, only to say, "He did not have his medallion. He always wore that medal."

Detective Mitchell knew exactly what Cindy was referring to. In fact, it was Detective Mitchell who awarded Johnny the medal he wore around his neck and so close to his heart. That year, he saved a fellow classmate. Yes, Little Johnny's dream to become a hero came to full fruition. A younger student started to cross the street. She failed to look both ways. As such, she stepped into oncoming traffic. Johnny, seeing that her life was in peril, jumped in front of the vehicle only to shield her body from impact. Thankfully, the driver stopped. Both children were spared, and Little Johnny became the neighborhood champion!

"He was so proud of that award," his mother added. "He would never take it off." With that, she held her hand close to her mouth and continued to sob bitterly.

Meghan felt terribly helpless. How could she bring comfort to this mother who mourned for the miracle that Johnny brought to his family and community? To add to her feelings, how could she explain the twenty casualties that have now be drudged up? Words were, by far, beyond her comprehension.

Detective Oliver quickly chimed in, "Ma'am, we will do everything to find the person responsible for your son's…"

Cindy could not bear to hear the next word. She turned and started her ascent up the hill when the word she feared the most caught her ear: "Death."

Nature tried to recapture the beauty it lost as a light snow started to fall from the heavens.

CHAPTER

7

The weather complimented the mood of the people. It became quite ugly. Again, the soft flakes that descended from the clouds grew in mass and momentum. Detective Mitchell gazed to the heavens. For some strange reason, she believed that "nature was not finished unveiling its secrets."

"What are you trying to tell us?" she mumbled.

"What did you ask?" Detective Oliver questioned. "Are you speaking to me?"

"No. I was thinking out loud," Meghan replied.

"So, what were you thinking?" Oliver inquired.

"Is this an interrogation or a test?" Meghan asked.

"Neither. I was only asking, " Oliver rebounded.

Meghan's emotions were mixed. She was irritated with her father. For him to undermine her abilities was incomprehensible. Yet, she was thankful. To have Detective Oliver lead, of all cases, this case was more of a help than a hindrance. But, then again, the knowledge of twenty dead bodies on her turf and under her watch was daunting.

Meghan attempted to sort through her thoughts. "Well, Detective," she went on to say. "It seems to me that nature is trying very hard to tell us its secrets."

Curious about her response, Oliver had to know. "What do you mean nature is trying to uncover its secrets?" He then added, "You would think it would want to keep its secrets buried."

"Yes, a person would think so. But my instincts are telling me the woods have more to reveal."

"Really? So, what are your instincts telling you?" Oliver asked.

"I am not quite sure. My gut is telling me the killer is here watching us. He or she is before us at present."

Impressed by Mitchell's answer, Oliver went on to add: "Your instincts are probably correct. Did you know the majority of killers aid and assist in the investigation? They want to see the direction of the case. Oftentimes, they leave little hints and trinkets to confuse law enforcement."

"Yes, yes I do," Mitchell countered. "I have read about several cases where the perpetrator became an active participant in the search and rescue process."

Oliver smirked and then smiled. He went on to say, "It seems that you have this case pretty much solved. I am not sure why your father bothered to trouble me."

"Oh come on, Detective. Do I detect some pride on your part?" Meghan inquired.

"Not at all," he said proudly. "For all you know, I can be the 'perp.'"

"That is nonsense in my book. If you need to be puffed up, then let me share how my father always spoke so highly of you."

Surprised by Meghan's response, Oliver had to feed his already fledging ego. "Really? What has your father said about me?"

"As a little girl, I remember my mother and father discussing some of their cases," Meghan shared. "I vividly recall my father talking about your instincts."

Meghan's voice started to soften. "It was not until Becky's death that I finally conceded that you were the best of the best." She paused for a long second and asked the question that troubled her for so many years. With a wounded heart from yesteryear, Meghan had to inquire, "Detective, do you believe Becky honestly died at the hands of her father?"

Puzzled by Meghan's question, Detective Oliver retorted, "That's a stupid question. Of course, I do. All the evidence pointed to him." Trying to dig a little deeper into Meghan's inquiry, Oliver raised his right eyebrow and countered, "What prompted you to ask me such a question? It was your father, wasn't it?"

"No, not really. It was my mother who questioned his innocence," Meghan shot back. "As far as she was concerned, there were some things about the case that didn't add up."

"So then, who is being interrogated? Me or you?" Oliver shot back.

Sensing Oliver's frustration, Mitchell did not hesitate to put him against the ropes. "What crawled up your ass and died? My mother had many questions about the case that did not make sense." She went on to add,

"Remember, she was a personal friend and his attorney."

Detective Oliver, irritated and agitated, was quick to answer the question asked, "So what was it that didn't equate with your mother? I did everything I could to solve the case."

She continued her train of thought, "If you must know, you arrogant son of a bitch, my mother questioned the timeframe displayed before the jurors."

"What in the hell does that have to do with anything?" Oliver snorted.

"My mother," Meghan went on to explain, "didn't know how Becky's father could commit such an atrocity when records indicated that he was serving a citation for a traffic violation."

"Shit, Detective!" Oliver snarled. "I don't have the time or the energy to explain everything. If your mother had any quarrels with my investigation, she should have brought it before the court!"

"She did, you asshole! What I don't understand, Detective, is your defensiveness. If you did your job, then how is it that this case, Becky's case, is getting under your skin?"

Realizing his indiscretions, Detective Oliver backed down and backed off. "You are right. I did everything according to the book. Everything and every piece of evidence pointed to Becky's father." Almost apologetically, Oliver went on to say, "Look, we have twenty murders to solve. Whether we argue over the past or we focus on the present is entirely up to you."

Finally, both detectives came to a consensus. Meghan responded with, "At least we can agree on this point. We need to get moving, let's go!"

"Remind me again" Oliver snickered, "who's leading this investigation, me or you?"

"You are. So, I need you to set your testosterone aside and start taking the lead."

Oliver, still simmering over Meghan's previous comments, had to ask,

"Out of curiosity, Detective, where would you begin?"

"I would begin with Johnny's disappearance," she said confidently.

"What would make you begin with Little Johnny's death?"

Before Meghan could explain her reasoning, news crews came rushing toward both detectives. They saw the heated discussion between them. "Detectives!" one reporter shouted. "What is your next move?"

Oliver tried to regain whatever ground he lost with Meghan. He attempted to put himself in the national spotlight. His efforts were squashed when Meghan pushed him to the side and answered the question asked. "We are going to start with the disappearance and death of Little Johnny."

"Why Little Johnny?" another reported blurted.

"Because he is the most recent of the twenty victims," Meghan added. "Until we know who the other victims are, then we must concentrate our efforts on what we do know."

Another news anchor chimed in. "What are your thoughts about these cases?"

Detective Oliver was once again the center of attention. He raised his hand to answer the question but was rudely interrupted when the news received word of another letter sent to officials. Another body was found in another park. He was dumbfounded. He was perplexed. His reaction was somewhat uncharacteristic of a man who devoted his life to fighting crime. Though most people did not notice his unusual behavior, Meghan did. She was not sure if he was more perturbed that his time with the press was curtailed or that another murder had taken place.

Meghan sensed his disappointment. Politely, she apologized, "Our deepest sympathies go out to all families." It was she who now was earning respect with the press and the public. "However, me and the lead detective, Oliver, need to get busy about our business. If you want to and must know, yes, there is a serial killer on the loose." She concluded her claim to fame when she added, "We will do everything we can to solve these cases. Thank you."

CHAPTER

8

Oliver and Mitchell cut through the crowds. The once snow-covered land instantly turned into ice. Cautiously, they ascended the hill now deemed unsafe only to be knocked back down to the river's edge. Oliver fell first, and like a stack of dominoes, he took those behind him. Thankfully, he was the only person to feel the full force of the fall. He tumbled backward. He fell liken to a rock rolling down a hill, tossing and turning, all the while gaining momentum. He abruptly came to a halt when the law of inertia guided him to the river below. The splash from his tumble sent a ripple effect across the crime scene. It was felt by all.

He popped tall. His clothes were drenched. He was more than pissed. As if Meghan's repertoire with the press wasn't enough to soak his ego, now to have this "slideshow" further drown his reputation. Oliver could literally feel his claim to fame slipping through his fingers.

He looked to the top of the ravine and shouted, "Would somebody throw down a damn rope large enough to pull us up!" Oliver noticed that cameramen were recording his slip from glory. "Turn those damn cameras off," he blurted. "This investigation is about the victims and not me!"

Meghan did not help matters. When she saw her partner draped in anger and dripping wet, she started to laugh. "It serves you right! You had it coming to you."

"What do you find so funny and what in the hell is that suppose to mean?" Oliver angrily asked.

Detective Mitchell had her partner right where she wanted him. "Most people would call that karma."

Before Oliver could say anything, Detective Mitchell put the icing on the cake when she added, "You can wait for that rope all day long. As for me, I can and will climb these banks without any assistance."

Shocked by Mitchell's somewhat disrespect for authority, Oliver countered, "Then what?"

"I will meet you at the station," Meghan responded. "Another homicide has been added to our list. Maybe this one could offer some fresh leads."

Then, like a snake, she slithered up the hill. She used whatever means available to conquer whatever obstacles in front of her. She grabbed trees when needed, and she used her fingers to support the treads of her boots as they tried to bite in the frozen soil.

Detective Oliver stood there. He was beyond words. He was stupefied. No longer was he steering the helm, Meghan was. In an act of desperation, he reiterated his previous order. "Would someone throw down a damn rope! I have work to do."

CHAPTER

9

Meghan came to an abrupt halt when she noticed something laying on top of the snow's surface. It was a medal of sorts. In fact, it was Johnny's medal. *How can this be?* she thought. If anything, his medal should have been buried deep beneath the snow-covered hills. Yet, there it was. It shone as brightly as the day she first pinned it to his shirt.

Immediately, she knew the killer was amongst them. She looked hard and long at the footprints left behind. The only prints that seemed to correspond to the location of Johnny's treasure were none other than Detective Oliver's. It was there that he lost his footing and sported his acrobatics. Sharply, Meghan looked down only to see her partner still standing in the riverbed all the while screaming out orders for someone to cast a rope.

The freezing rain and temperatures compared nothing to the frostbite that stole her soul. "This can't be," she murmured. "Or could it?" For the sake of Little Johnny and the other twenty victims, it was a question worth investigating. Meghan quickly snatched Little Johnny's medal from the frozen ground and placed it in her coat's front right pocket.

She proceeded to mount the icy slopes of the ravine. The moment her feet hit solid ground, she found an agent from the Crime Scene Unit. Softly, she requested that Johnny's medallion be examined for fingerprints and DNA. She made it clear that no one, and she meant no one, was to know of her findings or the results. Though the examiner wondered if a report should be submitted to Detective Oliver, Meghan reiterated her previous request. No person was to know. She had her suspicions, suspicions that were meant to be kept under wraps.

Before returning to the station, Meghan walked to the ravine's edge. There she saw Detective Oliver digging into one of his front pockets. By all appearances, it seemed he lost something. She could see the frustration mounting on his face. She squinted only to capture Oliver's lips muttering the word *shit!* The moment that word spewed from his mouth, he looked up. It was then that both detectives' eyes zeroed in on one another.

Meghan took a step back. Something was not right with this picture. A chill ran down her spine. Like her counterpart, she too echoed the same word he had spoken a second or two ago. "Shit!"

CHAPTER

10

On her way to the station, Meghan could not concentrate. Her mind spiraled out of control. To think that a fellow officer was responsible for so many deaths was beyond comprehension. She tried so hard to make sense of the situation now staring her in the face. *How could it be?* she thought. *It has to be. Detective Oliver was the only person remotely close to where Johnny's medal lay silently and lifelessly on the surface of the snow. Yet, it screamed out for justice. And what was he looking for deep within his pockets? It must have been Johnny's medal.*

Meghan held the steering wheel as if her life depended on it. Her emotions got the best of her especially when she remembered her last encounter with Becky and Little Johnny. She sobbed uncontrollably. She steered her vehicle to the roadside. She pounded the wheel clinging for some sort of stability. She let loose of the anger boiling within her as she blurted out, "You did not die in vain! I will find the person responsible for taking your lives."

She quickly buried her head in her hands. "What am I to do next?" she whispered aloud.

Her answer came more quickly than expected. Someone was knocking on her driver's side window. It was Detective Oliver. Trying to hold back the tears, Meghan rolled down her window. Softly, she asked, "What do you want?"

"Come on, Detective," he said firmly. "We have work to do. The chief wants us both at his office, pronto!"

She wiped the tears streaming down her face, Meghan acknowledged and agreed to Oliver's request. "I'll be right behind you." She looked at his clothes. They were still drenched and softly responded, "Shouldn't you get dried off before pneumonia sets in?"

For a man who lost all composure at the crime scene, Detective Oliver showed a compassionate side of himself. "I will change when I get to the station. My concern is more for your well-being. Are you sure you want to proceed with this investigation?"

"Yes, yes, I am!" Mitchell said somewhat confidently. "There are so many questions that need answered. It's difficult for me to digest."

Oliver's response caught Meghan off guard. "Believe me, I understand. In all my years as an investigator, never have I seen such a scene."

For a moment, Detective Mitchell let her guard down. "Really? I thought you were immune from such atrocities."

"I hear that too much," he said sympathetically. "But a person with a glimpse of a conscience can never become accustomed or acclimated to the loss of life."

Mitchell's heart almost melted. That is until Detective Oliver followed his statement with another question. "By the way, did you happen to find anything when you climbed the ravine?"

Whatever impressions Meghan had for her partner were absorbed in his already drenched attire. "What are you talking about?"

"I noticed how you retrieved something midway through your triathlon up the hill?"

Mitchell's shield quickly went on guard. "I do not know what you are referring to?"

"Oh, come on, Detective," Oliver said. "I saw you lean over to retrieve something. Don't play with me, what did you find?"

"It was nothing, sir," Meghan said. "Why do ask?"

"I lost something very personal to me, that's all," Oliver countered.

"With all due respect, sir," Mitchell said, "I am not in a position to dictate what I retrieved. It could be something but, then again, it could be nothing. We will have to wait and see."

Meghan's apprehensions were magnified when Oliver made a statement that ran contrary to their investigation. "Okay!" he blurted. "If you want to play hardball, then it is hardball we will play. In the end, you will be the one who suffers, not me!"

"What in the hell is that supposed to mean?"

"You will see," Oliver snided. Meghan was intimidated by his glare and his gestures. "It has been my experience," Oliver went on to say, "that the truth will make itself known. It's only a matter of time."

Agitated by Oliver's demeanor, Detective Mitchell reminded him of the tasks before them. "Look! There are twenty-one unsolved cases we must attend to. I do not have the time arguing over the tits for tats. We will discuss this particular subject at a different time and place. Right now, we must focus our attention on the facts presented to us."

Before Oliver could say anything, Meghan, without much hesitation but with much provocation, put her car in drive and sped away.

CHAPTER

11

It was difficult for Meghan to park her car at the station. News crews from around the country violated every law that protected spaces for officers, employees, and the handicapped. Her father had finished his press release and was on his way to his office when Meghan burst through the crowds, the press, and the doors of the precinct.

"Dad!" she blurted. "There are some things we need to discuss!"

The chief, aggravated by his previous press conference, tried to remain composed. "Look, Detective, when it comes to police work, I would appreciate you remember my position rather than our personal relationship. I already have enough riding on my shoulders. Do you understand?"

"Yes, sir!" Meghan shouted out.

Staring his daughter in the eyes, the chief asked, "So, what is on your mind, Detective?"

"Well, sir, I am somewhat hesitant about…" Mitchell started to say. That is until Oliver stormed through the chief's door. His wet clothes started to dry. They clung to his body as if they were now a part of his skin.

The chief looked at him in bewilderment. "What in Sam's hell happened to you?"

Oliver was quick to respond. "Never mind, sir! Another homicide?" Oliver questioned. "You got to be kidding me!"

"No, it's not a joke, and I am not laughing. This morning, I received another letter from our killer. Like previous ones, it was quite explicit and detailed." Trying to catch his breath and his frame of mind, the chief went on to explain, "I have already sent a unit to the scene. They confirmed everything the killer expressed in the letter. What I need from you is to begin investigating this killing apart from the others. Apparently, our killer went beyond our jurisdiction."

"But, Chief—" Meghan went on to say, only to be interrupted.

"Look, I really don't have time for your questions. I want answers," he desperately said. "Since Detective Oliver has jurisdictional privileges, I want him to investigate the latest murder," the chief clearly articulated. "As for you, I want you to further your inquiries about the other victims."

"With all due respect, sir," Meghan pleaded. "Don't you think that is a little too much for one detective?"

"Probably. But what choice do I have? We have twenty corpses in our own backwoods, and now we have been taxed with another body outside our perimeters."

"We can get another agency involved," Meghan said somewhat sympathetically.

What the chief said came as no surprise. "Not on my watch, Detective. Now I want Oliver to trace down any leads of the last victim. As for you, I want you to start with Little Johnny's death and work backward."

Meghan's expression said it all. She was overwhelmed. She was frustrated. The task placed on her shoulders seemed too much. There, father and daughter stood staring one another down. Neither one was budging on their respective positions.

Oliver broke the silence between them. "Chief, I agree with Detective Mitchell. What you are requesting is too much for any one person. May I suggest that I investigate this recent murder and compare my findings with Little Johnny's death. There has to be some connection between the two."

"That's a great idea!" the chief said somewhat frantically. "I want you both to dig up as much pay dirt by tomorrow morning. By that time," the chief added, "the coroner should have some preliminary reports for you to unearth."

"I am glad you two can come to some sort of consensus, but, sir," Meghan shouted, "there are some things I desperately need to discuss with you."

Sensing the urgency in Mitchell's voice, the chief conceded to the detective's concern. "Very well," he said. He stretched forth his hand and handed Oliver everything regarding the last murder. "Oliver, here is the information. Do what you do best, Detective."

"Yes, sir," Oliver complied. "With all due respect," he went on to say, "may I shower and change my clothing?"

"Your request is granted," the chief said. "You look like crap!"

With that, Oliver rushed out of the chief's office as quickly as he stormed in. He went to his car, retrieved his suitcase, and then proceeded to get cleaned up.

CHAPTER

12

Meghan allowed her passion and persistence to get the best of her. She slammed the chief's door only to blurt out, "I know today has been difficult and draining, but it has not been easy for me either."

Dazzled by his daughter's actions and attitude, the chief countered with, "What do you know about difficulty?"

"Sir!" the young detective shot back. "I know that today is the twentieth anniversary of when Becky's body was discovered. I know today her father dies for a crime I believe he did not commit." Tears started to flow steadily down her cheeks. "How dare you question me about how I feel and what I am suppose to feel! Becky was my best friend, or did you forget?"

The chief, setting all professionalism aside, reached out to Meghan. He wrapped his sturdy arms around her. He cradled her as if she were a newborn and offered words of compassion. "You are right," he whispered. "It is wrong for me to think that you were not affected by Becky's death. Please, I ask, forgive me."

There was a long pause in this moment made for television. It took a few moments before he realized the gravity of what his young detective was trying to say. "What do you mean that Becky's father was not responsible?"

Meghan first planted her face in her father's shoulder. She followed that gesture by pushing him away. Her actions were truly indicative of the struggle waging within. Smacking him on the shoulder, she continued her thoughts. "You know, Dad, I mean, Chief, you can be a real butthead at times."

In an attempt to try to change the tone, the chief somewhat chuckled.

"That's always been my job."

"As a father or a chief?" Meghan asked.

"Both. So, tell me what makes you believe Becky's father is innocent?" He hesitated for a few seconds and started to sob. She knew the bonds both men developed over their years in law enforcement. She also understood how it ripped her father's heart out to arrest him for such a heinous crime. "You know there is nothing we can to do stop his execution?"

Now it was Meghan who cupped her father in her arms. "I know, Dad. But what we can make amends by catching the person responsible."

In a soft voice, the chief had to ask, "Who do you think was responsible?"

"Oh, Dad! If you only knew what I thought." Meghan struggled to spit out the rest of her sentence. The mere thought sent shockwaves through her body. "I am almost convinced that Becky's killer is also our serial killer."

Puzzled by his young detective's intuition, the chief sought to further his own investigation. "What makes you think there is a correlation? How do you know?"

"I don't have the time to go into great detail," Meghan said, and then asked, "but don't you think it's ironic how twenty souls were found on our turf? And how the twenty-first was brought to our attention on exactly the same day when Becky's father is to be executed?" Catching her breath, she added, "Father, you always taught me that there are no such things as coincidences."

Reluctantly, the chief gave his young detective the green light to move forward with her instincts. "Okay. I trust you. All I ask is for you to keep me informed about your progress."

"Chief, I would expect nothing less but to honor your request." Meghan gave her father one last hug and then exited the station. The news were still scrambling to find their way in this remote part of the country and still trying to script whatever events were soon to unfold.

Their cameras zeroed in on Meghan leaving the scene. "Excuse me," one reporter inquired, "is there anything you have to share regarding the disappearances and deaths of the twenty-one victims?"

Detective Mitchell tried to skirt the issue, that is until she heard one newscaster ask, "Detective! Is it true that these murders are tied to the murder of your friend from year's past?"

Meghan's momentum came to an abrupt halt. She turned to the person asking the question. She looked into the cameras only to abruptly answer the question asked. "Look!" she demanded. "At this point in our investigation, there is no need for anyone to draw parallels from a murder that occurred twenty years ago to the others before us."

The young detective heard another reporter ask, "What exactly is that suppose to mean?"

Mitchell went to respond when the chief came bursting through the doors.

He could hear the commotion outside. It was his intention to divert any and all attention away from his detective. Before she could answer the question, the chief said in a moment of passion and in a way to protect his detective, "We already had a press conference pertaining to the murders now placed on our plate." He went on to add, "Our detectives are actively and aggressively pursuing all leads. We will keep you informed to details made available to us. At this time, I respectively request that you let my team do their jobs."

Hoping he quenched any suspicions, the chief was shocked when an up-and-coming anchorman stretched the question, "But, Chief, do the people of this small community have a reason for concern?"

Attempting to distract this fledgling newscaster, the chief gave a curt answer, "As I said in my initial press conference, there is still much for us to discover. Until we get the coroner's report, we cannot infer any correlation between one murder to the next." Almost apologetically, he concluded his statement with, "Now let my detectives do their work." The chief turned away from the "swarm of bees" hovering below. He was halfway through the doors of the station when this young reporter, whom most experts considered green behind the ears, shouted, "What are you trying to hide?"

There was a sudden hush in the air. The chief stopped. Like a seconds hand paces steadily around the face of a clock, the chief turned in sync with each of its ticking. He looked directly into the crowd. He pointed his finger directly to the place where a projectile had been fired.

"Son!" he commanded. "What is your name, boy?"

"Anthony, sir."

"Let me tell you something. I hope you never forget what I am about to say," the chief countered and then continued, "I have been doing police work while you were still crapping green. Don't you ever question my abilities to do the task before me or behind. Do you understand?"

Anthony knew he pushed the peripheries, but that was not going to stop him from his inquisition to this bullheaded chief. "Chief!" Anthony blurted, "Who are you trying to protect?"

That question pushed the envelope. The chief had enough. His response was demonstrated more by frustration than restraint. He started to hurdle over the rail. One of his officers wrapped his arms around the chief, offering words of reassurance. "It's not worth it, Chief," the officer said. "You have enough to deal with. You do not need to add to an already full plate, sir."

The officer's words cushioned the blow this young reporter was soon to experience. He let loose of the chief. The chief regained his composure. He tucked in his disheveled shirt. He then glared into the eyes of the young reporter as if to say, *We are not finished.*

CHAPTER

13

Detective Oliver drove to the site where the last body was found. It was only a few miles outside of the chief's jurisdiction, but far enough to pull the investigation in a different direction.

Oliver immediately started his inquiries. He quickly discovered that this victim had a name. It was Rachel. She had disappeared some days ago. Though teams gathered to search for her, their attempts were unsuccessful. Like Little Johnny, she, too, was laid to rest in the deepest of ravines. Her body was covered by the elements of nature.

On further inquiry, he was somewhat stunned by the many similarities of this victim to Little Johnny, yet shocked by the dissimilarities. For instance, it was not a coincidence that both victims were last seen riding their bikes through the area, nor was it mere chance that they were only children.

There was something else eerily similar. Not so much between Rachel and Little Johnny, but she and Becky. Both girls were sexually assaulted. The instrument used in both cases was a foreign object, such as a broom handle or some other instrument circular in nature. In both cases, wood fibers were found in the vaginal area. For Becky, that was not information privy to her parents and the public. It was evidence that Detective Oliver could not easily dismiss. Of all people, he was fully cognizant of both crimes.

His curiosity piqued. He had to know. Therefore, he had to ask if the crime scene unit could determine which hand was used to thrust the object into Rachel's privates. It was somewhat a peculiar question, not to mention an awkward one. But Detective Oliver had his suspicions. His suspicions were dwarfed when the crime scene technician responded contrary to Oliver's instincts.

"Sir," the technician replied, "based on the evidence before us, we can only surmise that the perpetrator was lefthanded." Somewhat perplexed by the detective's question, the technician had to know. "Sir, pardon me for asking, but is that pertinent to this case?"

Although it was not the answer Oliver expected, he did what he did best.

He diverted the question. "I am doing what I am paid to do: ask questions and solve crimes. Is there anything I should know?"

"Nothing that I am aware of," the technician answered and then continued, "except…"

Agitated, Oliver was quick on the draw. "Except what?" The team leader did not have enough time to catch his breath when Oliver continued to drill him. "Come on, spit it out."

"Sir, we were informed that she always carried her teddy bear. We have yet to discover the bear along with her bike."

Oliver, still distraught that the total sum of his instincts did not equal zero, replied, "Very well. Keep me informed about any additional evidence you and your team dig up."

Returning to his vehicle, Oliver was rapidly enveloped by the media, where he found himself in the spotlight once again.

The first question came from Anthony, the aspiring journalist seeking to stake his claim to fame. "Detective, is there anything you would like to share with the citizens of these two communities?"

Regardless of his spill down the slippery slopes from the previous crime scene, Oliver was now on top of the mountain. "Yes, I want to reassure all residents that we will be actively and aggressively pursuing all leads. We will find the person or persons responsible for the crimes that now litter their backyards."

Seizing his opportunity to trip up this seasoned soldier, Anthony dug a little deeper. "With all due respect, it seems to me the chief is somewhat stonewalling the investigation."

With cameras rolling, Detective Oliver did not hesitate to steal the show. Anguished by the reporter's comment, Oliver stared into the eyes of this young reporter. "Excuse me," he blurted. "What are you suggesting, young man?"

Confident in his own intuitions, Anthony aimed his sights at Oliver and shot, "If truth be told, sir, I left the police station some moments ago." He continued his statement with, "I asked a simple question only to be almost assaulted and accosted. Had it not been for another officer to pull the chief back, who knows how the situation may have played."

Oliver's angst quickly turned into anger. He shot back. "Young man!" he exclaimed. "Do you understand the stress placed on the chief's shoulders?"

"I could not possibly imagine what must be going through his mind at this time," Anthony said somewhat sympathetically.

Oliver pointed his finger as if to take aim at the young reporter. He pulled the trigger and fired back, "Well then, you do not know the character of the chief, now, do you? Before you start wagging your tail and spouting off your tongue to make a name for yourself, I would strongly suggest you take the fifth…that is, keep your damn mouth shut! You will not find a nobler man than the chief!" Glaring into Anthony's eyes, the Oliver finished his assault by asking, "Do you understand me, young man?"

Anthony backed off and away. Somewhat regretfully and reluctantly, he responded, "Yes, sir."

"Very well, then," the old-timer shot a second round. "We have a lot of work before us. I promise we will do everything to keep everyone informed."

CHAPTER

14

Meghan did as the chief instructed. She returned to Henry's and Cindy's. It was a source of contention. It was one thing to have hope that Little Johnny would someday be found alive; it was quite another to know the harsh realities of his death.

Rather than parking in the driveway, she opted to pull alongside the curb. She steadily looked at Johnny's house. She remembered the first time she interviewed Henry and Cindy. If that was not difficult enough, this interview would be even more demanding. It was now a fact, Little Johnny was dead. His life was taken by someone whose mind could not differentiate or appreciate the difference between life and death.

She looked in the living room window. She could see Henry walking toward Cindy. By all appearances, he was trying to comfort her. Meghan could see Cindy. She had her head buried between her hands. It was also apparent that her tear ducts had run dry. Whatever reservoirs had ran dry.

Meghan knew that this was not an easy task. She knew the pain she suffered compared nothing to Henry's and Cindy's.

She quietly slipped from her vehicle as if not to awaken a sleeping lion. Silently, she walked to the front door and softly knocked. Though it was apparent they were home, Meghan prayed they did not answer. This, by far, was not where she wanted to be.

Henry slowly opened the door. Hesitantly, he welcomed Meghan in his home. "You know this day has been very difficult," he said, pausing between thoughts. "We know what brings you here, and we know you are doing your job." He took a long sigh followed by, "Please come in."

Meghan stepped in. Out of respect, she politely slipped off her shoes. Henry escorted her to the living room. Cindy excused herself. She walked to the foyer and ascended the stairway to the second floor. She then did what she done when Little Johnny first disappeared. She opened the door to his bedroom. The reservoir that ran dry some moments ago found an unearthed spring. Tears broke through the dam. There was no controlling or stopping them. They came effortlessly. Cindy buried her head in Little Johnny's pillow. She prayed for the nightmare to end. She pleaded for her pain and sorrow to stop. Each of her tears came to symbolize her shattered heart. The truth about her little boy was now unveiled for all to see.

Her Little Johnny was now a fatal statistic. The mere thought of his death was too much for any mother. If she could not have her Little Johnny in her life, then life was not worth living. *How?* she thought. *How could God give she and Henry such a blessing, only to have him swept away?* There was not rationale or reason.

Henry did his best to remain composed. He knew Detective Mitchell would ask the same questions she did a year ago. He also understood she had a job to do. Meghan did everything she could to be sensitive to the emotional, spiritual, and physical status of Johnny's father.

Apologetically, she asked, "Is there anything you can recall that may shed new light on..." She paused for a moment and drew in a deep breath. Before she could finish her line of questioning, Henry interrupted and completed her sentence.

Tearfully, he responded, "On Johnny's disappearance?" The reality of the situation came rushing toward him like a raging bull rushes toward a matador. He softly rephrased his question with, "His death?"

Meghan wanted to reach out to offer her support, but protocol dictated she not. She did everything she could to restrain the waters that were soon to break through the barriers of professional etiquette and personal experience. "Yes," she whispered ever so gingerly.

Henry reached for his handkerchief. He dried his eyes followed by clearing his nose. "I am so sorry," he said. "This has been a very difficult day for me and Cindy." He stopped to regain whatever breath remaining in his lungs. His only hope was that, that was the only breath he ever took. Unfortunately, life continued.

After a few moments of awkward silence, Henry finally found the strength to break through his heart's deepest and darkest desire to finish his sentence. "Outside of the unmarked police car patrolling the neighborhood, there is nothing else for me to add."

Henry then fixed his eyes on a family photo taken a month prior to his son's disappearance. He then asked a question that sent Detective Mitchell in a tailspin. "By chance, did your detectives happen to find Johnny's medal?

He was so proud of it!"

Meghan was beside herself. How was she to answer his question? *Of course I found it*, she thought. *But how could I honestly answer his inquiry without exposing the truth?*

Whether it was instinct or intuition, who knows? But what came from her lips next was comparable to a seasoned detective. "Henry, I promise our forensic experts are examining every piece of evidence found thus far."

Henry was not sure how to interpret her answer. *Did they find Johnny's medal or did they not?* he wondered. His facial expressions said it all. Meghan knew her answer was vague, but she also knew the less she said, the better off Little Johnny's parents were.

She reached out to comfort Henry's concern. She clasped his hands with hers. "Henry, I cannot imagine how difficult this must be for you and Cindy. Trust me, we are doing everything tied to your son's death." Her mood shifted from a personal friend to a professional crimefighter. "Is there anything else you remember about the day Johnny disappeared?"

"No, no there isn't," he remorsefully said. In an attempt to fight off his emotions, he politely ended his conversation with Meghan. Empathetically, he said, "My wife needs my presence. Please excuse me as I tend to her at this time."

"I understand, Henry," Meghan responded. "She needs you as much as you need her. I will keep you informed about any progress made in Johnny's case."

Henry bowed his head toward the floor. She was not sure if he wanted to pray or if he desired to be with his son. One thing was for certain, someone pierced a hole in Henry's and Cindy's heart. Despite advancements in science and medicine, Meghan knew there was nothing to ease their hurt.

CHAPTER

15

Detective Oliver drove to Rachel's home. Cars littered the streets as family and friends offered their condolences. Most people would have thought Oliver's investigation was an intrusion of sorts, but everyone in this small community wanted answers. He was cordially invited in and then escorted to Rachel's parents, William and Wendy.

They went to the parlor for more privacy. William and Wendy sat on the love seat while Oliver was offered the recliner opposite of them. The silence between the three was tense. William and Wendy knew what drew the detective to their home. They knew the harsh reality that their little girl would no longer be returning. They knew the pain would never cease. They knew a killer had to be caught, captured, and convicted.

Likewise, Oliver knew the severity of the situation. He knew that twenty-one bodies had been unearthed from their resting places. He wondered whether there was a definitive link between them. All he had was instincts, and what his instincts were digging up were not good. Before he said a word, he looked out the window. In the distance, he could see the woods where Rachel's body had been laid to rest.

The gentle rain turned into a light snowfall. Nature, once again, seemed to do everything to cover its secrets. All Oliver could do was stare. Even he was clueless about the events of that day. Never did he have to face the harsh facts that twenty-one souls died at and by the hand of some maniac. At present, three of those souls were children. He had yet to learn about the other victims. The mere thought was more than daunting: it was damning. He was lost. He was without any type of direction or discernment. Again, all he had was a hunch, a dog biscuit of sorts. He was truly banking that his canine instincts would not lose its scent.

It was Rachel's father, William, who pointed Oliver on the right course. It was he who started the interview. Not trying to disrupt Oliver's train of thought, William softly asked, "Excuse me, Detective. I am sure you have some questions for us."

Oliver's mind snapped to reality when William finally broke the ice. "Of course," he said sympathetically. "I know this must be taxing on you. I will do everything I can without spending any more of your time than necessary." Oliver paused. "Is there anything you can tell me about the day Rachel disappeared."

William and Wendy froze. By all accounts, that day was not any different than any other. Rachel, they went on to explain, was to walk to a friend's house. She, along with some other girls, planned on a sleepover. Rachel wanted to first stop by a neighbor's home before finishing her conquest. Though William and Wendy wanted to drive her, she opted to weather the elements outside. That day, snow fell from the heavens. Rachel could not wait to make her imprint on the fresh white powder. She hoped there was enough snow for her create angel or two along the way. Besides, she had her favorite stuffed animal to protect her.

"Do you know whether she made it to her first stop?" Oliver queried.

"Yes, yes she did," William stated. "As a matter fact, the family was our first point of contact when Rachel did not make it to her desired destination."

Wendy finally broke her state of frozenness by questioning her decision to let Rachel walk alone. "It's all my fault," she cried. "I knew I should have driven her. I just knew it, but…" William and Oliver sensed the guilt Wendy now bore. Had she taken Rachel to her friend's house, then this conversation would never be happening. Rachel would be safe from harm and at home.

In an attempt to dig a little further, both men asked, "But what?"

Oliver was not prepared for what he heard next. Wendy went on to explain, "But there was an unmarked police vehicle driving the streets."

Placing his shovel in the hole he started, Oliver continued, "How could you be so sure it was an unmarked police car?"

"Oh, come on, Detective," Wendy shot back somewhat sarcastically. "Who doesn't know an unmarked vehicle when spotted?"

"Please entertain me for a second or two," Oliver said while placing his foot on the shovel's spade. "Can you be a little more explicit about the car you saw?"

Wendy went from sarcastic to sorrowful. "If it is going to help…" She started to cry. The floodgates could not stop the water that washed down her cheeks. A deep hole pierced her very core. The once impenetrable walls of her heart were now spewing with grief. "Well, if you must know, the car was a white four-door sedan. It had black tires with simple hubcaps. And if that is not quite enough proof, the car sported a spotlight atop the driver's side roof and had governmental plates."

Oliver's tail went up. His instincts seemed to point in the same direction. It was not by mere chance that two vehicles with the same characteristics should be spotted on the dates of two disappearances. "Did you happen to get a glance at the driver?" Oliver questioned.

"No, not really," Wendy added. "Now that I think about it, the driver's appearance seemed somewhat suspicious to me."

"Could you please elaborate on your suspicions ?" Oliver dug a little deeper.

Thinking about it, Wendy started to sob uncontrollably. "Had I only known," she murmured to herself. "I should have done something."

Looking for pay dirt, Oliver had to thrust his shovel a bit deeper. "Had you known what?" he asked. "Please tell me what should you have done?" he begged.

Wendy's grief turned into guilt. "It's my fault!" she cried out. "It's all my fault! Rachel, forgive me. Please forgive me!" She threw her head into William's shoulder. It did not take long for Wendy's tears to saturate his shirt.

"Honey," he firmly said. "You need to let the detective know what you saw." He placed his hands on her shoulders and gently pulled her head away from his chest. He, like Wendy, was vulnerable. His little girl was now dead. Though he could not disguise his pain, his pain defined his strength. "Wendy, please tell him what you saw."

Wendy wiped the tears from her eyes and cleared her throat. "That afternoon," she said, "I came home from work a few minutes early. Rachel was in her bedroom getting ready for her 'big night out,' as she called it. She was so excited. It was the first time we allowed her to stay over at a friend's house."

William interrupted her story when he hastily blurted out, "I don't think that's what the detective desires. Dammit! He wants to know about the driver in the car. For heaven's sake, tell him."

By all appearances, Wendy was not the only parent struggling with guilt. William wrestled with it as well. His guilt, however, was coupled with anger.

Agitated by Wendy's lack of cooperation, William again expressed his frustrations. "Will you just tell the detective what he needs to know?"

Like a referee separating two boxers, Oliver stepped in. "Would it help if I asked some questions?"

Wendy complied to his suggestion. With her head now buried in her hands, she nodded.

"Very well," Oliver said with the utmost care. "Was the person a male or female?"

Baffled by Oliver's line of inquiry, Wendy whispered, "I don't know. That's part of the problem."

"Take your time." Oliver soon proved his worth as he continued to dig a little deeper into Wendy's recollection. "What was it about the driver that makes you question the gender?"

Immediately, Wendy remembered. She lifted her head from her palms and continued to give details about the driver. "It seemed that the person behind the wheel did everything to disguise his or her sex."

Hoping to sift through the dirt already dug, Oliver went on to ask, "What tipped you off?"

"At first glance," Wendy shared, "I thought it was a man. But when the car came closer to our house, it appeared to be a female posing herself as a man."

"You are doing great," Oliver said reassuringly. "Were you able to determine the person's gender?"

"No, not really. If I were to guess, I would guess it was a female."

"What would drive you to that conclusion?" Oliver probed a little further.

"There are some things a woman cannot disguise, such as her posture, her breasts, her hairstyle, her use of lipstick, and the way she handles the helm."

"Is there anything else you can remember about that day or the driver?"

Tears flooded her eyes as Wendy went on to confess, "I knew something was not right. My intuition told me not to let Rachel go." Sobbing uncontrollably, she added, "But she was so excited to stay the night at her friend's house. Something told me that I should have driven her there."

William's anger raged within. "What?" he shouted. "You mean to tell me that our little girl is dead because you decided to do nothing when you felt something?"

"I am so, so sorry," Wendy faintly said. "I let you and our baby down."

"Bullshit! I don't accept your apology, especially for this," William countered. "You are her mother. It was your job to protect our little girl!"

Oliver knew he may have dug a little too deep. "I believe I have heard enough," he calmly said. "Sir, if I may have a moment of your time, I need to speak to you privately. Ma'am, you may leave the room."

Wendy stood up and sheepishly exited the room. Oliver then took complete control over the matter. "Sir," he said with authority, "your wife does not need to carry any more guilt than what is already on her shoulders. She is not to blame for your daughter's death. Your wife needs you as much as you need her. Now go and be the husband I know you to be." With those final words, Oliver excused himself from the parlor and then the premises.

CHAPTER

16

The following morning, both detectives reported to the chief. His appearance was anything but professional. He had yet to leave the station. He had yet to shower and shave. He had yet to find some much needed sleep. Since Becky's father was to be executed at midnight, he remained at his desk until he received word from prison officials. It was the first and only time in his extensive career that his investigation led to a conviction and execution of a criminal.

At 12:10 a.m., his phone rang. While he knew the contents of the call, he picked up his receiver. Becky's father was declared dead at precisely 12:03 a.m. The chief did not say a word. He sat in complete silence and darkness. The solemnness of the room seemed to compliment his mood: silent and dark. His mind raced from twenty years past to the present.

In total, twenty-two bodies were dead. They all perished on "his watch." Though many of the casualties could have occurred in different jurisdictions, it did not matter. They all were strategically placed on his turf.

He could not escape his earlier conversation with Meghan. *What if Becky's father was not the perpetrator?* he thought. *If that's true, then an innocent man, a fellow officer, and a personal friend died for a crime he did not commit.* A whirlwind of emotions spiraled through him. To add to the velocity was the coroner's preliminary reports. He had yet to open the files. He was afraid to and, quite honestly, he did not want to. That he would leave to his detectives.

There they stood, yet the chief was oblivious to their presence. Giving the chief a few moments to let the storm within his soul pass, Oliver finally stilled the winds by clearing his throat. "Sir," he asked, "are those the coroner's preliminary reports?"

Before the chief could speak, Oliver snatched them from the desk. He started thumbing through each case. Thankfully, the coroner was able to give some basic information such as the ages of each victim, their gender, race, and cause of death. Oliver fell back in the chair seated behind him. His curiosity peaked with each profile.

Finally, he spoke out, "I can't believe it! We are dealing with a person who started her killing spree as a child!"

"What in Sam's hell are you talking about?" the chief shouted. "Look, Oliver, I know you are the best of the best, but I really do not have time for your bullshit right now."

"Chief, there is no bullshit about it! The killer started at an early and unbelievably, he is a she! Sir, I know you are tired and overwhelmed, but the facts do speak for themselves."

Meghan jumped in the crap match between the seasoned officers. "How can you be so sure with so little information to go on?"

Oliver snapped back. He was still steaming from the fiasco the day prior. "I have experience. I have instincts. And what I have before me is a profile of a female serial killer."

The chief shot back, "That is nothing more than nonsense! I respect your talent, but you are wrong about this one, Detective."

"So, Chief," referring to Anthony's question the day before, "what are you trying to hide?"

The chief's blood rushed directly to his head. A volcano was about to erupt and erupt it did. "Nothing, you cocky son of a bitch! How dare you even question me regarding this matter!"

"Remind me," Oliver said sarcastically, "who called who? You called me. Remember, you dumbass."

The chief's words were nothing more than lava flowing from the stress and strain he endured from the time Little Johnny's body was found. The chief slammed his fists against his desk. "Consider yourself off the case. Get out of here!"

Meghan chimed in. "Excuse me, Detective. What were you searching for in your front pockets yesterday?"

Oliver was stunned. He was puzzled by her line of question. "What in the hell are you talking about?"

"Yesterday," Meghan confidently said, "when you embarrassed yourself before me and the rest of the world, I saw you looking for something in your front pocket. What was it?"

The old-time detective snapped at the young detective like a turtle snagged on a fisherman's line. "That is none of your damn business, young lady." He took a bite when he added, "I don't have to answer to you or anybody for that matter."

Abiding by the chief's command, Oliver stood up and headed toward the door. "Chief, it's your ass on the line, not mine," Oliver said snidely. "I have another crime to investigate."

Oliver went to open the door when the chief barked out, "Detective! Those reports stay with me."

"Don't you dare talk to me like a dog. You want these files, Chief. Then fetch!" Oliver flung the files like a frisbee. Pertinent information flew across the office and on the floor. "There, dumbass. You and your protégé figure this one out."

Oliver stormed through the doors of the precinct. He noticed the media setting up their stations for the chief's interview soon to come. From the crowds of reporters, he spotted Anthony. He did not waste any time. He rushed to the side of this up and coming newscaster. He grabbed him by the arm only to say, "If you want a story to kick off your career, then it's in your best interest to come with me."

Anthony heard about Oliver's track record. He did not question. He only followed.

CHAPTER 17

The only thing to pierce the silence was the door slamming. The only thing the chief and Meghan saw was Oliver's ass walking out.

Befuddled by what had transpired, Meghan looked toward the chief in disbelief. "What in the hell was that all about?"

"Right now is not the time," the chief answered. "We have too much work ahead of us. Did you find anything of interest?"

Still in shock from what she witnessed, Meghan spoke as if she was walking on thin ice. "As a matter of fact," she went on to explain, "there is." She attempted to recapture her thoughts.

"Well, Detective, spit it out! I don't have all day. I have another press conference in twenty minutes."

"Sir, I believe Oliver may be the serial killer," she replied somewhat reluctantly.

"That's absolutely absurd," the chief snarled. "There is no way in hell he committed those crimes." He continued, "Your hypothesis is as ludicrous as the one he offered moments ago."

Hoping to gain the chief's approval rating, Meghan exclaimed, "Hear me out for a moment."

"Okay then, let me hear what you have to say! Remember, I don't have all day."

"Yesterday, I found Little Johnny's medal in the vicinity of where his body was discovered."

"So? A person would expect to find personal belongings near the crime scene," the chief responded.

"But that's not half of it."

Meghan tried to explain the other half when the chief blurted out, "Get to the damn point!"

"Could you at least show me some courtesy. I am getting there!" Meghan shouted. "At present, I don't give a rat's ass if you are my father, the chief, or the pope for that matter. My concern is focused on solving these murders."

"Are you done standing on your little soapbox?"

"Yes! I believe I am," the young detective said.

In her eyes, she proved her worth to be the lead investigator: a worth soon negated by the chief's remarks. "Then, by all means, Detective, get to the point!"

The chief's response knocked Meghan down a notch or two. But she was determined and relentless. She would drive her point home even if it meant pissing her father, the chief, or the pope off.

Instead of stooping low, she popped tall and spouted out, "Sir, you would think that Johnny's medal would be near his body, and rightfully so. However, when I found his medallion, it was laying on top of the freshly fallen snow that—" The chief went to interrupt the detective's train of thought only to be silenced before he could speak.

"Dammit! Let me finish, won't you?" Taking her ground, Meghan paused. "Thank you!" she exclaimed. "The only person remotely close to this discovery was none other than Detective Oliver. It must have fallen when he went tumbling to the ground and into the creek."

She had the chief's full attention on this point and at this point. "Really?" he inquired.

"Really! I gave the evidence to the chief crime investigator to test for DNA and fingerprints. I pray he has some results for me this morning."

"So, tell me, Detective, why are you still standing here?" the chief asked and then ordered, "Go! Get the hell out of here!"

CHAPTER

18

Oliver quickly whisked the young reporter to the passenger side of his squad car. "Get in!" he shouted. His mind was as dense as the fog looming over the land. He could not believe the chief would question his intuition, let alone his instincts.

Perplexed by the detective's behavior, Anthony countered with, "What in the hell is going on? The other day, you practically ripped a new asshole in me for asking a simple but pertinent question."

"Dammit! When will you learn to keep your mouth shut? If you want a story to kick off your career, then it is a story I will give you!" Oliver dictated.

Anthony was not sure how to react. He did as the detective ordered. That is, until Oliver drove everywhere, but went nowhere. Anthony's curiosity got the best of him. He had to know. His journalistic instincts kicked in. He had to ask, "Excuse me, Detective. Where are we going?"

"I'm getting my thoughts in order," Oliver shot back.

Uncertain whether he should speak or remain silent, Anthony opted for the latter. He sat silently. Oliver pulled the car off the side of the road. He was transfixed in thought. He completely forgot he was not alone. There, he spilled the beans. He vented his frustrations about the murders as well as the chief's ineptitude for connecting the dots.

Anthony listened and digested everything Oliver had to say. There did come a time when the detective opened the door—a door he wished he never opened. That door opened when Oliver questioned the chief's motives. "I don't know who or what he is trying to protect?" he said aloud.

Anthony, receptive to the detective's thoughts, asked, "Protect whom or what?"

Unbeknownst to Oliver, he answered, "I don't know. There are some things that do not make any sense. They don't add up!"

The detective was in a fog, and Anthony knew it. He knew Oliver was driving with his low beams on. No longer was he cognizant of the young reporter's presence. Anthony did what any aspiring journalist would do. He seized his opportunity. He probed, "Can you give me an example?"

"I know the murderer started her killing spree at an early age," Oliver whispered to himself.

"Her, sir?" With Oliver's visibility next to nil, Anthony's query only added to the dense precipitation clouding the detective's mind.

"Yes!" he blurted. "Yes, the evidence points to a female. I saw the reports. I am confident that he is really a she." He continued babbling and added, "I don't understand what prompted her to switch hands?"

Anthony now became part of the investigation. In as far as Oliver was concerned, Anthony was now his conscience. "Maybe she had some sort of injury." The seeds were now planted. They were planted in fertile soil. They would produce good fruit. And in the end, they proved their value in this market for a murderer.

Amazed at his conscience, Oliver shouted out, "Why did I not think of that sooner?"

"I don't know." Anthony softly said. His next thought seemed to lift the thick haze enveloping the detective's thoughts. "Maybe it was a sports injury? I would guess our killer was either athletic or committed to exercise."

Intrigued by the voice now speaking, Oliver continued to gather his thoughts. "What would lead you to that conclusion?"

"I don't know, sir. You saw the records. What makes you so sure it was a female?"

Though the thick cloud was starting to evaporate, Oliver still entertained this line of reasoning. "The means and methods used. Based on what I read, the majority of victims were sexually assaulted. The reports clearly indicated that penetration was made by some foreign object other than the obvious. If it was a man, he would have used the parts the good Lord had given him."

"How can you be so sure?" the voice resting in Oliver's thoughts asked.

"Could he have been impotent?"

"A person would think so," the detective said, "but everything I read points to a female perpetrator. There is no doubt in my mind. This murderer is a woman."

"Detective, are you sure?"

"Absolutely," Oliver answered. "I know what I saw. It is most definitely a she."

Anthony lost his edge when his next question penetrated the cloud looming in Oliver's thought processes. "For the record, sir…"

Oliver looked toward the passenger seat. He was shocked to see Anthony.

"How in the hell did you get here?"

The young reporter knew he crossed the line. He stared at the detective like a deer staring into headlights. Stuttering to find the appropriate response, the reporter only reported the causal chain of events. "Sir, I beg your pardon, but it was you who dragged me into this equation." Somewhat dumbfounded, he asked, "Don't you remember?"

"No, no I don't. My only recollection is when I challenged the chief regarding the coroner's preliminary findings. From that point on, my memory is nothing more than a blur."

"Well," the reporter went on to explain, "it was you who tossed me in the front seat. It was you who invited me to be a part of this investigation. It was you who asked if I was trying to make a name for myself." He looked at Oliver's reaction. He understood that this seasoned detective acted in ways atypical of a seasoned detective. "You don't remember, do you?"

Oliver did not entertain the question. Instead, he put the car in drive and returned to the road. Anthony's inquisitiveness got the best of him. He wanted to know. He needed to know. So, he asked, "Where are we going now?"

"To the place where I believe it all started."

The young reporter felt confident. Sadly, he misinterpreted the detective's motive. What Anthony thought was a meaningful conversation was doused by Oliver's next comments. "Either you watch, listen, and learn, or I drop your ass off the side of the road."

"But, I thought—" Anthony tried to explain only to be cut short by the detective.

"You thought wrong. I will let you know what you need to know and when you need to know it. Speaking of it, it would be in your best interest to keep your mouth shut and your eyes open."

CHAPTER

19

While Oliver and Anthony were in the process of building a bridge, Meghan and the chief stepped outside to nothing more than chaos.

Reporters captured Oliver kidnapping another reporter. The focus of their investigation now focused on the apprehension of one of their own.

"Chief!" one reporter shouted. "Can you enlighten us as to why your primary detective snatched a fellow journalist?"

Oblivious by what had taken place, the chief did his best to sidestep the issue at hand. "I don't know what would prompt Oliver to apprehend your colleague." Without thinking, the chief dropped a bomb on the press. Whatever apprehensions the news had about the case flung open. The chief revealed the contents of pandora's box. Clearing his throat, the chief made a startling announcement. "Detective Oliver is no longer part of this investigation," the chief muttered.

"Excuse me, sir!" one news anchor yelled. "What do you mean Oliver is no longer part of the investigation. Isn't he the best?"

Though the temperature outside was slightly above freezing, it was apparent by the evidence the chief was sweating. Whether it was the weather or the stress from being under the spotlight, no one was sure. What they did know is that Oliver was no longer leading the case. The chief started to recant his previous statement only to return to the original issue. "Where was Oliver?"

"Yes," the chief answered. "Yes, he was the best. He's served the city and our community well," he went on to explain. "But, at this time, his services are no longer valuable."

"What is that suppose to mean?" the news anchor followed. "Are you suggesting Oliver was involved in these crimes?"

Politics were never the chief's strong suit. He did everything to divert the question, but the press was relentless. The chief finally succumbed to the pressure. "All I can say is..." He hesitated for a moment. "Is that Detective Oliver needs to give an account to some of the evidence recently unearthed."

"Chief, a simple yes or no would have been sufficient," the reporter went on to say. "So, then, Anthony was not too far off the mark. You are hiding facts."

"That is not what I said," the chief contended.

"Could you please clarify exactly what you meant?" the reporter shot back. "Oliver snatched a reporter this morning. Do you believe he is in danger?"

"That, sir, I do not know." The chief aimed and then fired. The round he shot did little to dent the armor of the press. "All I can say is that Oliver was privy to some information not known to us. In regard to your colleague, all I can do is hope and pray for his safety."

"I'm sorry, Chief," the reporter said. "You keep dangling the bait before us. Answer the questions as asked."

Meghan could sense that her father was in treacherous waters. His preserver was failing, and it was failing miserably. There was no way she would let him become prey to the shark infested waters. She took a step forward only to throw out a lifeline. "As you can see," she said empathetically, "the chief already has enough on his plate. The last thing he needs is to be engulfed by predators of the deep."

"How are we to interpret what you said?" the reporter continued. "What are you trying to hide? Better yet, who are you trying to protect?"

"Nothing and no one," Meghan said. "We are pursuing any and all leads," she added. "At present, all we have is suspicions but no suspects."

This reporter would not let go. Sure, Meghan threw out a lifeline for the chief, but that was not enough to quiet his concerns. Like a shark pursuing its prey, this reporter was after blood. "My questions have yet to be answered," he bit.

Meghan struggled to thwart the attacks from the creature below. "What questions are you alluding to?"

In his attempt to deflate Meghan's ego, this reporter did not flinch to lunge toward the young detective. "Well, for beginners, to what extent does Oliver have in these investigations?"

Similar to the day before, Meghan stole the spotlight. She was arrogant, yet she was on point in answering questions. "Detective Oliver has been asked to step down from further investigations. As such, he has been excused from pursuing any leads to the cases before us."

"Detective," the reporter went on to add. "Is there any correlation between these homicides to Becky's?"

Meghan was caught off guard. Never did she expect anyone, a reporter for that matter, to draw the same conclusion as the detective relieved from the case. "What makes you think there is a correlation between them?" She went on to ask.

"Do we look stupid? Come on, give us break!" another reporter shouted. "Do you honestly expect us to believe there is a coincidence between the bodies found on the day of an execution? And let's not forget about the letters mailed to both the police and the press."

Trying to divert the reporter's attention, Megan reminded him about the law. "Sir, everything you cited is nothing more than circumstantial. At present, there is no evidence to either confirm this claim or claim it as nothing more than just a mere coincidence."

"Detective, you know as well as I do. Your last statement is nothing more than bullshit. There is no such thing as a coincidence, especially when it pertains to a serial killer."

The chief went to bat for his young detective. "We are presently looking into all leads. Detective Mitchell needs to return to the cases at hand. The moment any new information is fed to us, we will do all we can to throw you a bone. Thank you."

"But, Chief—" A reporter started to spill out, only to be turned by the chief's acquiescence. The chief was now protected by the doors that gently closed behind him. Meghan refused to entertain any more questions. She, like her father, remained silent. She turned a deaf ear to anything and everything that flew her way.

CHAPTER

20

Before Oliver confirmed his suspicions, he had to make one stop. Anthony sat still as this detective did what he did best. He was searching for answers. Unbelievably, he drove to the coroners.

Anthony finally broke the silence. "Detective, if I may ask—"

"You may not," the detective said. "Do as I instructed. Watch, listen, and learn. If you have a problem with my suggestions, who knows, you may very well become a cadaver."

"Was that a threat?"

"Well, smartass. What do you think?" Oliver answered. With a smirk on his face, the detective said, "I meant it as a forewarning." He stepped out of the car. He walked to the passenger side and tapped on the window. "Are you coming, or are you just going to sit there with your thumb up your ass?"

"I am coming, sir," Anthony responded somewhat hesitantly. "What do you want me to do?"

"Young man, it is your job to report the facts as presented. Anything less is a miscarriage of justice. Anything more is a violation of truth."

The detective headed toward the entry door when his gut feeling suggested that he was alone. He turned toward the car only to find Anthony still sitting.

"Are you coming with me or not?"

Anthony was literally beside himself. He did not know what to do or say. He paused for a moment or two. "We don't have all day." Oliver said.

"I know," the young reporter sheepishly confessed, "but I have yet to see a corpse, let alone an autopsy, sir."

Oliver was frustrated. He was not in the mood to mince words. "Look, there was a reason I picked you from the other reporters. Babysitting was not one of those reasons. Either you get your head out of your ass or sit there. At this point, I really don't give a shit."

Unannounced, Oliver burst through the office doors. The receptionist did not have a chance to check him in or the identity of the person who crashed through the office. He directed his rapid pace straight to the examination room. He could see the twenty-one victims sprawled out on the table in the order they were killed.

"What do you have for me?" he commanded. He looked at each victim. "Is this the order in which they died?"

"I'm sorry, Detective, but I have been told you are no longer on the case," the coroner reported.

"Word gets around now, doesn't it?" Oliver sarcastically asked.

"Detective, you know I cannot allow you to go any further than the lines you crossed," the coroner said. "You know the rules as well as I do."

"Yes, I understand," Oliver said. Over the years, this detective learned the loopholes in the legal system. He knew how to get the information he desired. "But I am not here to discuss the first twenty victims, but I do need to know about the twenty-first victim, Rachel."

The coroner did not have a leg to stand on. Rachel was out of the chief's jurisdiction. Oliver had every right by law to look for any evidence found on her. He knew exactly what the detective was up to. To get to Rachel's tattered body, Oliver had the green light to pass each of the preceding ones.

There, he and the coroner walked. When all was said and done, they crossed twenty corpses. Each corpse dying well before their time. The detective could not help but notice the development of the killer. The age of every cadaver was indicative of the murderer's growth patterns. In other words, as the murderer grew in age and stature, so too did the victims. That was precisely the key Oliver needed to break this case wide open.

"Interesting," he said beneath his breath. "Very interesting," the detective said out loud only to ask a question that seemed to have no relevance to the case. "Could you please pull the records from Becky's homicide?"

Confused by such a request, the coroner questioned the detective's motives. "How in the hell does that fit into these crimes? Do you know what you are doing?"

"I have a hunch, and I don't have time to explain," the detective added. "I have a suspicion that our time together will soon be interrupted."

The detective's instincts were spot on. The moment he finished his sentence, the door flung open. There the two detectives stood. The examiner was at a loss for words, but it was he who broke the ice. "Damn!" he exclaimed. "You are good."

Trying to gain control over this volatile situation, it was Meghan who struck the first match. "Why are you here? You are no longer part of this investigation." Adding fuel to the fire was Anthony. He was standing by her side.

Oliver's first reaction was to chuckle. "I should have known." His eyes were set on the young reporter. "Let me guess," he added. "You were busy calling Meghan when I insisted you follow me?"

Anthony shrugged his shoulders as if to deny any responsibility for his decision. "I was doing what I was told to do. Remember, dumbass, it was you who dragged me into this mess."

The seasoned smiled and then smirked. "Son of a bitch," he yelped. "I should have known. Well, Doc, it seems that I am not as good as you first suspected. I guess I am getting too old for this shit."

"That's enough for introductions and instincts," Meghan blurted out. "Detective, you are now ordered to leave these premises or surrender your credentials. Your services are not required."

The medical examiner's back was up against the wall. He was literally stuck between a hard spot and a rock. He first glanced toward Meghan and then Oliver. He had no choice but to concede to Mitchell's demands. He addressed the seasoned detective, "I am sorry. My only advice is to follow your instincts. They will lead you to the truth."

"For Pete's sake!" Meghan replied. "What in the hell is that suppose to mean?" Frustrated by Oliver's relentless pursuit, she glared first at the medical examiner and then to Oliver. "Don't encourage him! As far as I am concerned, he is washed up. Yesterday's mishap proved that."

The old-time detective refrained from participating in the "crap match." His experience dictated to remain calm, cool, and collected . He knew not to leak any more information to

Meghan and Anthony. He would lose his edge: that, in and of itself, was not worth sacrificing.

His next comments were directed to the coroner. "Thank you," he replied. "I am sure you know where you may find me."

The examiner did not need to say anything. With a simple nod, he acknowledged the detective's intuition.

CHAPTER

21

Oliver exited the room as quickly as he entered it. Meghan could not control herself. She had to know what drove the former detective to this scene. Staring the medical examiner directly in the eyes, she started her reign of terror. "Could you explain what he was doing here, and what prevented you from stopping him?"

The coroner took a moment to reflect. He thought carefully about the causal chain of events that led to Oliver's inquisition. "Well," he started to say, "I did everything to thwart his attempts. But…"

"But what?" Meghan blurted out.

"Please let me finish," the coroner begged. "I did everything to stop the detective. Unfortunately, the law was on his side. Rachel was the last body in line. Legally, he still had all rights to know the cause of her death."

"How does Becky's death fit into this?" she questioned.

"Apparently, he believes there is a connection between the two."

"Dammit! What gave you the right to entice him?"

Temperature in this frigid environment started to rise. The medical examiner saw and heard enough. Pointing his finger at Meghan, he exclaimed, "Don't talk to me in that manner! You know exactly what Oliver expects and where he is heading now. Detective Mitchell, enough is enough."

Anthony was not quite sure how to interpret what he heard. He did not know if he was following the wrong investigator or if, by chance, they were on to something bigger than what he hoped. In the heat of this fiery moment, when a person believed that even the dead would rise, he thought it best to see this case to the end.

Meghan diverted any suspicions when she inquired, "Did you find any trace evidence off Little Johnny's medal?"

"As a matter of fact, I did," he went on to say, "but I don't believe I have the 'smoking gun' you are looking for."

Somewhat stunned, Mitchell took a step back. "Did you find DNA on the medallion?" She was insistent and persistent. "Or fingerprints?"

"Yes, yes, I did. Unfortunately, it was your fingerprints," he answered.

In an attempt to divert the attention away from her, Mitchell countered with, "That should come as no surprise. I was the last person to touch it. I picked it up after 'sure foot Oliver' lost his footing on the hill."

"That was my first impression," the medical examiner said. "That is, until I did a little digging on my own."

"Digging!" Meghan shouted. "For what?" She took some time to recollect her thoughts. "Did you find what you were digging for?"

"I am not sure," he said.

"What is that suppose to mean?" the young detective blurted out in haste.

The doctor was careful how to explain the dirt he unearthed. "When I put the fingerprints in the database, the results were the same found twenty years earlier." He looked directly toward Meghan. "Detective, they were prints."

The reporter's ears perked up. He remembered Oliver's babbling about how the serial killer started her rampage as a youth.

Mitchell was caught off guard. She never expected or suspected that her fingerprints were linked to Becky's crime. Her heart pounded against her chest. She had difficulty breathing. The pain associated and surrounding Becky's death came to the forefront. The tears flowed effortlessly. The mere thought of her best friend's death was too much. To believe that someone was now accusing and aiming his sights on her involvement was terrifying; better yet, it was tantalizing.

She stormed from the county morgue's frigid confines out to the parking lot. Another wintery blast made its presence felt as a heavy snow started to fall. Meghan looked out to witness Mother Nature's beauty and power. Everything about that dark and dismal day was enveloped by the snow. She looked to the heavens and remembered a Psalm she learned as a child. It was a Psalm of David. Her father taught that particular verse shortly after Becky's death. Distraught, Meghan needed something to still her young soul. She blamed herself for her friend's demise.

There in the parking lot, she openly recited it word for word:

"Purge me with hyssop, and I shall be clean: wash me, and I shall be whiter than snow. Make me to hear joy and gladness; that the bones which thou hast broken may rejoice. Hide thy face from my sins, and blot out all mine iniquities.

Create in me a clean heart, O God; and renew a right spirit within me" (Psalm 51:7–10, KJV).

The same strength she received as a child was now with her. There was a peace that passed all understanding. She regrouped and regained the confidence she sought. She marched back into the room where death now laid. With the spirit of renewal on her, she looked into the eyes of the medical examiner and offered a valid explanation. "Of course, my fingerprints were found at Becky's crime scene. I was the last person to see her alive." She stood silent and paused, only to exclaim and explain, "The next time you start pointing fingers at suspects, get your damn facts in order."

"Detective," the examiner said, "I can only go where the evidence leads me."

"That's great!" she shouted. "Since you and Oliver seem to be on the same page, where is that old-timer headed?"

"If I were to guess, Detective Oliver is on his way where everything began," the doctor clearly stated.

"And where might that be?"

"You tell me. I was not around twenty years ago, but you were," the coroner exhorted.

Meghan wasted no time. She understood exactly where Oliver was heading. In her haste, she looked at Anthony. "Are you going to stand there or follow me?"

"I am behind you," he said. The young reporter was on Meghan's tail. He was determined to follow her footsteps, wherever those footsteps may lead.

CHAPTER

22

Oliver drove directly to the place where it all began. Unbelievably, it was the chief's old house. Since Becky was last seen with Meghan, Oliver realized the importance of retracing his steps. For the past twenty years, the house remained vacant, that is until someone recently purchased it. It was scheduled for demolition within the week.

He parked along the curb, exited his vehicle, and approached the house. He could hear dogs barking from a nearby residence. To avoid further distraction, this old-time detective did what he did best. He used the greatest trick known to man. He distracted the dogs. He threw a bone or two for them to fetch.

After the dogs settled on their treats, Oliver went to the back door. There, he used another trick in his arsenal of tricks. He slid a credit card between the lock and the door jamb where he quickly gained entry in Mitchell's home. He did not waste any time. He climbed the stairs like a rock climber climbs a mountain. He took one step at a time. He went directly to the place where, if his suspicions were correct, he would strike gold. And he was not disappointed.

He knew the layout of the house. And why shouldn't he? He often frequented the chief and family on special occasions. He also knew that most serial killers were apt to build shrines in a place near and dear to their heart. Usually, it is a room adjacent to the master bedroom. Not to awaken or arouse whatever dragons that may be hiding, he approached the door with extreme caution.

Steadily, he reached his hand toward the knob only to find it locked. Time was of the essence. His experience dictated that visitors would soon crash his party. With one thrust, he kicked the door open.

His heart literally melted as his instincts were finally confirmed. There, he saw a room dedicated and devoted to all the victims laying in the morgue. It was difficult for him to take in. Pictures and newspaper clippings wallpapered the walls. Each victim along with the articles of their disappearance was carefully placed in chronological order. It became quite apparent the progression of the killer: each age for person, each missing coincided with Meghan's development.

Words escaped him, and the air was knocked out of him. Whatever breath he caught was immediately sucked out of when he stood tall and turned to the opposite wall. Trophies of the victims were carefully placed in an enclosed case. At the top was the necklace Becky received on her tenth birthday. On the bottom was Rachel's teddy bear.

His knees immediately buckled. He bowed his head. *How could he allow such an atrocity to happen?* he thought. "I was the lead detective. I was the person responsible for convicting Becky's father," he cried. The thought that Becky's father died for a crime that he did not commit was overwhelming. But that thought did not compare to what was to come next.

With his knees offering support, Oliver looked up at the case now staring at him. He counted out loud the twenty-one lives lost because of his ineptitude.

Had he been correct in the beginning, then twenty-one lives may have been spared. He tried to reason and rationalize everything, but it was too much even for him to grasp. In an attempt to get his balance, he grabbed for a table to his right. His nightmare was not over. His hand lost its grip from a stack of magazines.

He fell forward. Using both hands to regain his balance, Oliver stood erect. He looked toward that table where he previously lost his edge. If his heart previously melted, it now sunk. Before his eyes were clippings from various subscriptions. The letters clipped were identical to those used to torment police officials. If that was not bad enough, his eye happened to catch two envelopes sitting on a table next to the magazines. They were addressed to the police and press. Along their uppermost edge were the words *catch me if you can*.

His attention was snapped. He heard a car pull in the driveway followed by the slamming of two doors. A voice from outside ordered, "Are you coming or not?" It was Meghan's voice. Oliver braced himself for what was to come. He remained in the room and patiently waited. His time as a legendary crime fighter was soon coming to an end.

CHAPTER

23

Oliver heard Meghan and Anthony make their way through the back door, across the kitchen, and up the stairs. A staredown and shootout of sorts was soon to take place. It was not quite the O. K. Corral, but in Oliver's mind, it was a close second.

The young detective and reporter entered the room where Oliver stood.

His back was facing them. He held up the two envelopes. "So," he started, "how much longer did you think you would get away with this?"

Meghan was surprised to see the two sealed envelopes dangling before her. It was not difficult for her to read the message sprawled across the top of both. "What in the hell are you talking about?"

Adding drama to this scene as it unfolded, Oliver remained with his back toward Meghan. That is until he heard the young detective draw and cock her weapon.

Slowly, he turned to face his one-time partner and now an adversary. He could sense the young detective's aggravation, especially in light of the smile that stretched across his face.

"You find this funny?" she asked.

"No," he said in an affirming yet authoritative voice. "But I always thought you were right-handed."

Meghan was suspect to Oliver's motives. Was he trying to distract or divert her attention? She was not sure. She recalled her father describing in great detail Oliver's tactics. At this point, she was not sure if he was employing another tactic from antiquity or if he was incorporating a different technique.

Frustrated, she answered the question asked. "I am, you dumbass! Why do you ask?"

"I don't know," he smirked. "Maybe it's because you are using your left hand to aim your weapon."

Without giving it a second thought, Mitchell slipped. She gave Oliver the information he so desperately needed. "I tore my right rotator cuff some years ago."

Finally, all the loose ends were tied. Oliver's gut feelings were confirmed. Everything added up. The aspiring reporter was correct. This killer did, in fact, suffer an injury. The correlation between the perpetrator and her victims coupled with the change of hands now made sense.

This interrogation came to a standstill when they heard the door of another vehicle slam its door. Oliver looked out and saw the chief. He laughed at the mere thought.

"What's so funny?" Meghan retorted. "I don't see the humor."

"It's your father," Oliver said sarcastically. "I guess he's here to bail your ass out again."

"Bail my ass out for what?"

"Oh, come on, you know as well as I do. Your father has bent over backwards to protect you." Regretfully, he went on to add, "Even at the expense of a family friend and fellow officer. I can't believe I fell for it: hook, line, and sinker."

The young detective didn't have a chance to respond. Before anyone could say another word, the chief rushed into the room only to show his age. He bent over gasping for air.

Oliver looked at the chief's condition and laughed. "It seems you have been sitting behind your desk too long."

"Shut up!" the chief snorted. "You never did know when to keep your mouth closed and your nose out of other's business." The chief stood up, all the while taking hold of his abdomen. Half-heartedly, he countered with, "But then again, it's all you have ever known. Which brings us here today."

Oliver did not waste any time to remind the chief of one simple fact. "We would not be in this damn predicament had you not involved me this investigation. What in the hell were you thinking, Chief? That I would not figure it out."

"Figure what out? You have not solved anything, you smartass, except how truly arrogant you are."

"Is that so? Explain this." Oliver then used his finger to direct the chief's attention to the clippings that lined the walls, the trophies neatly positioned in their case, and to the magazines sprawled across the nightstand.

The chief studied the pieces of evidence as presented. Though Oliver was proud of his findings, he was more than perturbed by the chief's response. "I'm sorry, but the only proof I see is nothing more than circumstantial. It will never hold up in a court of law. Besides, this home is scheduled to be destroyed. No one will ever know. Its contents will soon be buried."

Anthony decided to join the conversation. He was as dumbfounded as Oliver. "What are you saying? There is plenty of evidence to prove a person's guilt. I guess the question is, who is guilty, you or your daughter?"

Oliver's eyes lit up. His eyes turned right—right into the eyes of the chief. "You son of a bitch! How could you? How dare you?"

"I don't know what you are talking about!" the chief exclaimed. "You think I was the person responsible?" Shaking his head in disbelief, he added, "You are crazier than I thought."

"Dad!" Meghan screamed. "Stop it! Enough is enough!" She looked outside. Amazingly, snow started to fall from the heavens. She gazed toward the sky and softly whispered, "Purge me with hyssop, and I shall be clean: wash me, and I shall be whiter than snow."

For whatever reason, Meghan lost it. She started to sob. Whether it was the guilt she hid for so many years or the lies she lived, no one will ever know. "I am done, Dad! I can't do this anymore. I can't pretend. It's over!"

"That's right, sweetheart," the chief said ever so tenderly. "It is now over. No one has to know. It will be our secret." The chief did something that even Oliver did not see coming. He pulled his firearm from its holster and aimed it toward the detective.

"Let me now guess," Oliver calmly said. "You are going to kill me as well?" He looked deep and hard in the eyes of the chief. They were void of any life. Oliver understood what was to happen next. Whether it was Meghan or her father who committed twenty-one murders, it really did not matter. In either case, the old-time detective learned long ago that a father would do anything to protect his daughter, and a murderer would do anything to kill again.

The last thing Oliver saw was the chief's face. The last thing he heard was the click of a gun chamber. The last thing he felt was the burning sensation accompanied by a bullet piercing his chest. And the last thing he ever said was, "Shit." Blood steadily flowed from first the point of entry and then his mouth. It soiled the spot from where he once stood but now lay. Within a few moments, his life as a detective expired.

The chief approached his daughter. He did what any caring father would do. He embraced his little girl. "There, there," he whispered in her ear. "No one will ever know."

"Oh! Daddy," she softly said. "Why?"

"What are you talking about? Everything I did, I did for you," the chief said.

"But did Becky have to die?" Meghan asked. The pain she experienced was excruciating. It was fresh. She relived every moment of Becky's death. The mere thought of what happened on that fatal day was too much. She realized that even the snow could not hide their sins.

"Remember, sweetie, you wanted her necklace. I did everything I could to get one, but you couldn't wait." The chief let loose of his daughter. He walked toward the trophy case. He grabbed Rachel's teddy bear. He turned and presented it to Meghan. "Here, my little princess, I got this for you."

Meghan planted her head in the chief's shoulder. "But, Daddy, you know that's not what I wanted. I wanted Becky's necklace." She sobbed terribly. She loved her father. She admired him for as long as she could remember. "Daddy, will you please forgive me?"

Puzzled by her last statement, the chief pulled his little girl in tighter. He could sense something troubling her. "Honey, I don't understand. I have always forgiven you." The chief looked toward Anthony and asked, "What do you think we should do with him?"

She held onto him. "Daddy, don't you worry. I already have plans for him." Her next action completely caught him off guard. Meghan squeezed her father with all her might. Slowly, she reached down and retrieved her father's firearm. By the time he could react, it was too late. The gun discharged at point blank. The expression in his eyes clearly said every emotion possible: anger, hurt, surprise, betrayal, and, yes, forgiveness.

The bullet entered the chief's stomach and exited his spine. Paralysis was immediate. He fell next to Oliver. Both men were now face to face. The chief stared his old-time friend's lifeless eyes. He stretched his arm across Oliver's chest. Like Oliver, blood started to trickle from the corners of the chief's mouth. Before his heart discontinued its rhythmic drum, the chief softly slurred, "I'm sorry, buddy."

Meghan kneeled down to her father. She looked deeply into his eyes. His life had now expired. She smiled as she bid her farewells to the man who protected her over the years. "Daddy, I hope you can still forgive me." She kissed his forehead and offered him some advice. "What did you think I was going to do?"

She stood up. She glanced toward Anthony. There was no hint of remorse for the events that transpired. Confidently, she reminded him, "Didn't I tell you that we could knock off two birds in one spot?" The thought alone made her smile. "Did you buy the tickets?"

Filled with adrenaline, Anthony could not contain himself. Whereas the hearts of two men now stopped, his raced with excitement, "Yes, babe. Yes, I did."

"Good," she replied. "By chance, where are we going?" She had to ask. Life for her was about to begin in another place, in another time, and for another reason.

"It's a surprise, sweetheart," he added.

"You know how much I love surprises." Meghan headed to the trophy case. She opened it and gently reached in. Of all the trophies, it was Becky's necklace she desired the most. She removed it from its place among the top and tenderly pressed her lips against it. Anthony could faintly hear her words, "My daddy always told me that I would always remember my first." She thought for a second. "You know, he was right."

Anthony studied the room. Reality started to kick in. His adrenaline rush soon turned into fear. Not knowing what to do next, he had to know. "What do you want to do with the bodies?"

Meghan laughed out loud. "Oh, silly, don't you worry about it. The house has been inspected and approved for demolition. Sometime tomorrow, the wrecking crew is coming. Leave them lay. Let them be buried with the house."

Impressed with the details, Anthony felt more comfortable. Repented of any doubts he had, he applauded Meghan for her attention to detail. "You have thought of everything. How could I ever doubt you?"

"Now, let's get the hell out of here," she said with great enthusiasm. She walked toward Anthony. She took his hand. With their hands now clasped, they started to leave the premises with the aspirations of starting a new life. That is until Meghan remembered she had yet one other detail to complete.

"Wait right here, I forgot something." She slowly reentered the room.

Putting on a pair of latex gloves, she approached the men that now rested silently. She bent over to pick up the envelopes Oliver dropped. "I almost forgot," she said jokingly, "we need to stop by the post office."

She stood up and walked toward her new partner. She stepped over the corpses. She stopped. Something caught her attention. For a second or two, she thought for sure, Oliver's right hand started to twitch. She did a second take. From all appearances, he was just as deader than as he was moments ago. *It can't be*, she thought.

She and Anthony reunited under the door from where he stood. Hand in hand, they left together. Meghan could not believe her eyes when they stepped outside. The previous snowfall had literally covered all traces of any wrongdoings committed. Mother Nature once again shielded the past from its secrets.

All Meghan could recite were the words her father taught her years ago. "Purge me with hyssop, and I shall be clean: wash me, and I shall be whiter than snow."

ABOUT THE AUTHOR

The Whispering Woods is L. C. Markland's seventh novel. His other works include: *All Things Work Together for Good (Romans 8:28), Winds of Change, Hard to Say I'm Sorry, Whispers in the Willows, Killing Me Softly,* and *No Holds Barred: No Holding Back.* Though two of the novels, *All Things Work Together for Good (Romans 8:28)* and *No Holds Barred: No Holding Back*, lend themselves to sequels, this one has definitely been written for future series.

L. C. says, "It would be wrong for me to underestimate the power of encouragement. In 2014, I stepped down from my position as a pastor. At that time, I was plagued with pain as four back surgeries ultimately took their toll. My physical and emotional well-being were taxed beyond their limits. During such time, some friends encouraged me to start writing. Sure, I threatened and even entertained the thought, but never anticipated or even expected to write one, let alone seven."

Though his inspiration came from some great friends, it was his mother, Lucy Markland, who planted the seeds. She loved to read. In fact, she read every genre imaginable. His enthusiasm for literature stems from her. She always wanted to write a novel, but she didn't. She believed she lacked the education and experience to do so. Like any faithful son, he fulfilled her dream.

www.ingramcontent.com/pod-product-compliance
Ingram Content Group UK Ltd.
Pitfield, Milton Keynes, MK11 3LW, UK
UKHW022215230426
12048UKWH00016BA/862